The door to the hotel room opened.

Nathaniel slow___  ___ it was completely dark, h___ ___he room, closed the door, a___ ___ "I took a walk."

Nathaniel quic___ ___er for several moments befo___ _____ around Denver by yourself this late at night?"

Trying to ignore the fact that her husband was naked beneath the sheet, Agnes said, "I needed to think. Alone."

"Are you finished thinking? Alone?"

It was several moments before she nodded. It was several more moments before she said, "I almost bought a train ticket to California. Two things stopped me. The first thing was the fact that I didn't have any money."

"And the second?"

Agnes did not miss the desire in his eyes. She swallowed. "I- I want to be your wife." When Nathaniel let the sheet fall to his lap, she quickly added, "In name only."

Nathaniel shook his head. "You will be my wife in every sense of the word."

"That sounds rather medieval," she said, incredulously.

"I'm an old-fashioned man, Agnes."

"I know nothing about you."

"That makes two of us." He stared up at her for a moment before continuing, "We will talk later. Right now, I want to make love to you."

Agnes couldn't breathe. "You are definitely no man of God," she whispered.

"You have no idea."

When Agnes wrinkled her brow, Nathaniel continued, "I am a man, Agnes. Being a minister is just my occupation." He held out his hand. "Will you be my wife in every sense of the word?" Smiling a strained smile, he continued, "If you don't want to be my wife in every sense of the word, I will give you the money to buy a one-way ticket to California."

INTRODUCTION

The night I saw *High Noon* on the big screen was the night that changed my life forever - for the better. I was mesmerized the moment the late, great Tex Ritter (Father of the late, great John Ritter) started singing the opening notes to the movie's theme song *Do Not Forsake Me, Oh My Darlin'*, a song that became a running, haunting score throughout the film. I fell in love with the story and the setting of *High Noon*. I booed the bad guys, and I cursed the townspeople. My heart ached when no one would help Gary Cooper defeat the bad guys, and raced when the only person who helped him was Grace Kelly - who was against violence because of her religion. I loved watching a young Lloyd Bridges deal with his confliction - whether or not to help Gary Cooper. Aside from Gary Cooper, my favorite character was that of saloon owner, and Cooper's ex-lover, played by the beautiful, Mexican actress Katy Jurado. It was Katy's meaty role that helped me to create the role of my own saloon owner heroine, Julia.

Because of *High Noon*, I decided to create a ten-book western romance series set in 1880's Colorado. It was not my intention to self-publish my series. Blogging was good enough for me. Until I woke up one morning, and thought, I want to self-publish - thanks to my dear, dear friend, Peggy Miller, who passed away in 2008. Peggy and I shared a love for romance novels, and she told me about her self-publishing stint - which had cost her an arm and a leg. Thanks to her, I knew it was the only way to go - as long as it was cheap (er). And you were right, Dear Peggy - Everything turned out to be more than OK. It turned out to be wonderful.

Thanks to my love for westerns in both books and movies, I feel like I have the experience to tell stories that are just as good - maybe even better. When I write, I write as if the reader will be reading a film. My stories are filled with rich settings, dialogue, and conflict, rich characters - good and bad - whose stories are begging to be told. But more importantly, my stories are not just about romance and sex. My stories are about love, family, and community.

I chose to self-publish because it was the only way I could be in control. I didn't want my voice to be lost. I didn't want my vision for my cover art to be lost. Good stories come from editing, but great stories come from the author's heart and soul.

Thunder Mountain Brides has been a long, exciting challenge, and it'll continue to be a long, exciting challenge. I hope it will continue to live in your memory as a great western series long after the sun has set.

I would love to hear your thoughts on my books - my series. You can share your thoughts on my website at www.thundermountainbrides.webnode.com.

Happy Trails, Dudes and Dudettes!

-Amanda A. Brooks

THUNDER MOUNTAIN BRIDES

HIDDEN SECRETS
AGNES

by
Amanda A. Brooks

aab
PUBLISHING

Thunder Mountain Brides
Brooks, Amanda A. - 1974-
Copyright © 2011 Amanda A. Brooks
Cover art work Copyright © Amanda A. Brooks, 2011

cover art/book layout: DigiRetouch.com
editor: Rie McGaha
printed in the United States of America: CreateSpace.com

All rights reserved. No part of this book may be used or reproduced in any manner whatsoever without written permission except in the case of brief quotations embodied in critical articles or reviews. Without limiting the rights under copyright reserved above, no part of this publication may be reproduced, stored in or introduced into a retrieval system, or transmitted, in any form, or by any means (electronic, mechanical, photocopying, recording, or otherwise), without the prior written permission of both the copyright owner and the above publisher of this book.

PUBLISHER'S NOTE
This is a work of fiction. Names, characters, places, and incidents either are the product of the author's imagination or are used fictitiously, and any resemblance to actual persons, living or dead, business establishments, events, or locales is entirely coincidental.

The scanning, uploading, and distribution of this book via the Internet or via any other means without the permission of the publisher is illegal and punishable by law. Please purchase only authorized electronic editions, and do not participate in or encourage electronic piracy of copyrighted materials. Your support of the author's rights is appreciated.

FOR MORE INFORMATION, PLEASE CONTACT ME AT MY WEBSITE:
www.thundermountainbrides.webnode.com

Library of Congress Catalogue Number:

ISBN: 1460910974
EAN: 978-1460910979

aab Publishing
www.thundermountainbrides.webnode.com

DEDICATED TO

Peggy Miller

*for planting the self-publishing seed in my brain
and encouraging me to follow my dream.
I miss you.*

ACKNOWLEDGMENTS and AUTHOR'S NOTES

To Marjorie Parsons - www.digiretouch.com - You continue to amaze me with your beautiful covers. Thank you for bringing my Agnes and Nathaniel to life.

To Rie McGaha - You continue to make my words better, and my voice stronger. Thank you for helping me to become bolder and more daring with just a touch of naughty thrown in.

A very special thank you to Gary Simonian. Gary, thank you for taking your free time to help me with the production of my books and my website. Thank you for all your support, and knowing what's best for me. I couldn't have done this without you.

Thank you to Chris Rossen for agreeing to be my Nathaniel, and for giving me the exact poses I needed. And a special thank you to Jeannine Simonian for being my Agnes, and for sending me beautiful, wonderful photos. My Agnes wouldn't have been the same without you.

And thank you, Mom, Dad, Chanin, and Warren for supporting my dream. Your loving support means everything to me. Dad, thank you for getting several copies of Edith when it came out. Warren, thank you for getting copies for you and your Mom. Chanin, thank you for getting my book so you can be a character in my next one. And Mom, your words meant everything to me. I hope I made you proud.

SCENE SELECTIONS

Non-believer (1)
Now is not the time (1)
Crude and daring (2)
Only for love (2)
Marriage arrangement (3)
A sister's guidance (3)
The retiring room (4)
The advertisement (5)
The beggar (5)
Train to Thunder Mountain, Colorado (6)
Nick West (7)
Different from New York (7)
Sleeping in the church (7)
"Hearth and home" (8)
Something to hide (9)
An angel with a secret (10)
Interview (11)
New sheriff? (11)
A talk between two outlaws (12)
The cooking position (13)
The Sunday school teacher position (13)
Questioning Agnes (14)
The morning after (15)
A Thunder Mountain, Colorado snowfall (15)
Little Women (15)
Attending church (16)
In danger (16)
Ambushed by an Indian (17)
Suicidal (18)
That went well. (19)
Sorry (20)
Unfinished business (20)
Advisement (21)
Trust (21)
Sisters (22)
Once an outlaw, always an outlaw (23)
Leaving town (24)
Defending a friend (26)
Cowboy Dave (27)
Thunder Mountain square dance (27)
Refusing punch to a prostitute (28)
Beautiful soiled dove (29)
Solitaire (29)
Moonshine (29)
Counting down to 1881 (30)
To hell with propriety! (31)
Last kiss (32)
The kiss (33)
No time! (33)
Reasons (34)
I am a Jew. (34)
God didn't make mistakes (36)
Consensus (36)
A friend in Miss Cooper (37)
Proposal (38)
Because I want you. (39)
On the train to marriage (40)
It will be a cold day in hell before I sleep with you! (40)
Bread without butter (42)
A bigot (42)
California or me? (43)
Who am I to judge? (45)
You murdered me, Nick! (46)
Revealing their pasts in their own time (46)
Being watched (47)
The new Mrs. West (47)
Why is it...? (48)
Giving her the truth (49)
There's something rotten in the State of Denmark (50)
Why did it hurt so much? (51)
Support (51)
I heed your warning, my lovely little outlaw. (52)
Violence, religion, and love (53)
Alone (55)
Why can't you be Nathaniel's wife? (56)
Why hadn't she believed? (58)
We must find Rachel before he does! (58)
Marriage announcement (59)
Tonight! (59)
Order (60)
Town 9 Prepare to die!!! (60)
Thou shalt not kill (62)
What about love? (64)
Make me! (65)
Of love. (67)
Boot Hill (68)
Fuck! (68)
Resign (69)
Miss Mabel's confession (71)
I love you, Miss Mabel. (72)
Found (72)
No escape (73)
Drowning (74)
Saving Agnes (75)
Tallulah's blessing (77)
Blessed and whole (77)
Family reunion (78)
Moonshine wedding (79)
Name your fool. (79)
Sunset kiss (80)

"I have learned silence from the talkative, tolerance from the intolerant, and kindness from the unkind; yet strangely, I am ungrateful to these teachers."

-Kahlil Gibran

Name: *Agnes Rachel Crandall*
Date of birth: *January 31, 1857*
Place of birth: *Brooklyn Heights, Brooklyn, New York*

CHAPTER ONE

Non-Believer

Brooklyn Heights, Brooklyn, New York
November 20, 1880

Rachel "Agnes" Berezovsky wanted to be anywhere but where she was. Staring up at the high, decorative ceiling of *Brooklyn Heights Temple*, she sighed audibly.

Embarrassed, Rivkah Berezovsky gave her daughter a warning glance.

Turning away from her mother, Agnes continued to stare up at the ceiling. Such exquisiteness meant nothing to her. How could it mean anything to her when it had been created out of wealth?

When the other women stood to sing the final prayer, Agnes stood, too. She closed her eyes, but did not lift up her voice in prayer. How could she?

She did not believe.

Now Is Not The Time

Agnes and her two younger sisters finished preparing the tables for supper. Sneaking a red grape from the bowl, Agnes popped it into her mouth, and entered the kitchen.

Rivkah Berezovsky looked up from the dessert she was putting the finishing touches on, and simply stared at her second eldest daughter for a moment before saying, "I am not happy with your attitude, Rachel."

Rolling her dark eyes, Agnes said, "Now is not the time to discuss this, Mother."

"I agree, Rachel. First thing tomorrow morning, your father and I will be sitting down with you to discuss not only your attitude, but your future."

"You and Father need not bother. It's no secret the two of you are very disappointed in me."

Rivkah Berezovsky glanced at the cook, who was pretending to mind her own business. "You were right the first time, Rachel. Now is not the time to discuss this."

Agnes stormed out of the kitchen.

Looking down at the dessert, Rivkah Berezovsky closed her eyes.

CRUDE AND DARING

Agnes did not like the way young Rabbi Jacob Kuhn was staring at her. Lifting her glass, she took a sip of cold water, and looked down at her uneaten plate of food.

Agnes was no fool. She knew why Rabbi Kuhn had been invited to Sabbath supper. Deciding to have a little fun with him, she smiled, and asked, "Tell me, Rabbi Kuhn, is sex more pleasurable when one is circumcised?"

Ignoring the shocked gasps of those around her, she popped a red grape into her mouth.

Rabbi Jacob Kuhn stared at her for a moment before warning, "You will refrain from being so crude and daring when you are my wife, Miss Berezovsky!"

Glaring at him, Agnes coldly exclaimed, "I will never marry you, Rabbi Kuhn!"

She quickly stood, knocking over her chair, and hurried out of the dining room.

ONLY FOR LOVE

Sharon and Joanna sat on the edge of their elder sister's bed, and took her hands in theirs.

"Are you all right?" Sharon asked her.

"Not really," Agnes said, staring down at her sheeted lap. "While I don't regret having said what I said, I know I'll be facing the consequences of my actions tomorrow."

"You're a brave soul, Agnes," Joanna said.

Smiling shakily, Agnes said, "I was a lot braver earlier."

"It would be so much easier if you would just marry Rabbi Kuhn, Agnes," Sharon said.

Agnes and Joanna stared incredulously at their sister.

"How can you say such a thing, Sharon?" Joanna exclaimed.

Agnes let go of her sisters' hands, and quickly got out of bed. Walking over to the floor-to-ceiling windows, she looked out on her now-quiet Brooklyn Heights neighborhood.

After several long moments, she said, with fierce passion, "I will run away before I allow Father and Mother to choose my husband for me!" Turning to face her sisters, she continued, in a softer tone, "I will only marry for love."

Marriage Arrangement

November 21, 1880

"What are you doing here?"

"Rachel Agnes Berezovsky, you will apologize this instant for your rude behavior!" Rivkah Berezovsky ordered.

Agnes did the exact opposite. She sat down on the sofa across from Rabbi Kuhn, and glared at him. In a nicer tone, she repeated, "What are you doing here, Rabbi Kuhn?"

Placing his coffee cup and saucer on the coffee table before him, Rabbi Kuhn said, "I came here to finalize our marriage arrangement."

Agnes turned as white as a ghost. "Wh- What?"

Smiling, Rabbi Kuhn said, "You heard me, Miss Berezovsky. I originally planned for the wedding to be on the Saturday before your birthday, but under the circumstances, I have decided we will be married on Saturday, the fourth of December. Two weeks should be sufficient time to prepare for the wedding."

"It will be a cold day in hell before I marry you, Rabbi Kuhn!"

Rabbi Viktor Berezovsky grabbed his daughter's arm, and forced her to stand. "You have gone too far, Rachel! Apologize!"

Breaking free from her father's grasp, Agnes ran out of the parlor.

Rabbi Jacob Kuhn stood. "I suggest locking her in her bedchamber until the wedding."

While Rivkah Berezovsky just stared at him, Rabbi Berezovsky said, "Done."

A Sister's Guidance

November 24, 1880

Agnes looked up from her book when her very pregnant sister, Rebecca, entered the bedchamber.

Slowly sitting on the edge of her bed, Rebecca looked at her for a moment before saying, "It is time for you to respect our religion, and our parents, Rachel."

Rolling her dark eyes, Agnes returned to her book.

Rebecca grabbed the book from her sister's hands, and tossed it across the room. "It is time for you to respect me, Rachel!"

Agnes quickly sat up, and glared at her. "You are not my mother!"

"I may not be your mother, but I am your sister. As the eldest, it is my duty to protect and guide you, Sharon, and Joanna."

"I'm twenty-three. I do not need your protection, nor your guidance, Rebecca."

"You are unmarried."

Agnes stood, and went to the windows. "You make being unmarried sound like a crime."

"It is a woman's duty to marry and bear children."

Agnes glanced at her sister's protruding stomach for a moment. "I refuse to live in a loveless marriage."

"You need to learn to think before you speak!"

"I will not apologize for who I am, Rebecca. I refuse to marry Rabbi Kuhn. Father and Mother cannot make me marry that man. And neither can God!"

THE RETIRING ROOM

December 3, 1880

"You don't need to use the chamber pot, do you?"

Agnes shushed her sister.

"Are you going to run away?"

"Be quiet, Joanna!"

Agnes and Joanna made their way down the empty hallway of the temple toward the retiring room. Just as they reached the door, Rabbi Kuhn stepped out of the shadows, startling them.

"Going somewhere, ladies?" he asked.

Unsuccessful at hiding her nervousness, Joanna said, "We- We are going to the retiring room."

Rabbi Kuhn stared at them for a moment. "I want to speak to you, Miss Berezovsky." Looking at Agnes, he continued, "Alone."

After Joanna hurried into the retiring room, Agnes leaned against the wall, and closed her eyes.

"What are you about, Rachel?"

Agnes opened her eyes. "What do you mean?"

"If you think to run away, think again."

"I don't know what you're talking about."

Rabbi Kuhn took hold of her chin with one large hand, forcing her to look at him.

"No more games, Rachel! Come tomorrow night, you will be my wife in every sense of the word. If you dare to embarrass me, I will make you suffer! Do I make myself clear?"

Frightened, she whispered, "Yes."

"I will escort you and Joanna back to the services."

"I- I need to use the retiring room."

Rabbi Kuhn stared down at her for a long moment before saying, "Five minutes."

He leaned against the wall, and patiently waited the five minutes he allowed his bride-to-be.

When an extra few minutes had passed, an impatient Rabbi Kuhn entered the retiring room to find Joanna washing her hands, while nervously chewing her lip. The overly decorated room was cold due to the open window.

His defiant bride-to-be was nowhere to be found.

THE ADVERTISEMENT

Manhattan, New York
December 5, 1880

Cold and frightened, Agnes stood against the wall in a filthy alley, eating a stolen hot potato.

Although exhausted, she knew she had to keep moving.

It was only a matter of time before they found her.

The stinging wind blew open the damp newspaper lying on the icy ground. Agnes kneeled down to read the advertisement for a Sunday school teacher in Thunder Mountain, Colorado.

Tearing the page out of the newspaper, she stuffed it into her bodice.

THE BEGGAR

December 6, 1880-Half past eight of the clock in the morning

Agnes was beginning to hate potatoes.

Nibbling on the stolen cold vegetable, she wondered how she was going to get on the noon train to Thunder Mountain, Colorado without a single cent to her name.

Although she had several hours until the train came, Agnes made her way toward the station. She refused to spend another second in the filthy Manhattan slums.

The sudden appearance of Rabbi Kuhn stopped her dead in her tracks.

Smiling evilly, he asked, "Did you think you could run from me, Rachel? Did you think I wouldn't find you? I am taking you back to the house, where my father will marry us. After the wedding, you will get food." He looked her over from head to toe before continuing, "Not to mention a hot bath. I refuse to bed you until you're scrubbed clean."

Agnes kneed him in the groin, and watched as he doubled over in pain.

Just then, a filthy beggar came up to them. He placed his hand on the rabbi's arm. "Can ye spare some change?"

Rabbi Kuhn shouted, "Get the hell away from me!"

Hurt, the beggar said, "I just want some food." He smiled sadly. "An' a drink."

Rabbi Kuhn glared at the beggar. "I said, get the hell away from me, you filthy scum!"

The beggar dug his long nails into the rabbi's arm.

Rabbi Kuhn took out his pocketknife, and quickly thrust it into the man's stomach.

With growing horror, Agnes watched as the beggar collapsed to the ground. It was only a matter of time before the poor man expired.

"You- You murdered him!"

"He was just a filthy beggar," Rabbi Kuhn said. "No one will miss him."

Tears streamed down her face as she watched the old man painfully die. She then stared incredulously at the man who had just become a murderer.

He held out his hand to her. "Come, Rachel. It is time to go home."

Distaste written all over her face, she said through clenched teeth, "Go to hell!"

Rabbi Kuhn took a menacing step toward her.

Without hesitation, Agnes ran for her life.

Despite the pain shooting through his groin, Rabbi Kuhn chased her until the pain overcame him.

Furious, he watched as his bride-to-be disappeared into the crowd.

TRAIN TO THUNDER MOUNTAIN, COLORADO

Boston, Massachusetts
December 6, 1880-That evening

Nearly knocking down a dark-haired woman, Agnes ran hell bent for leather toward the train bound for Thunder Mountain, Colorado.

CHAPTER TWO

николас West

Nick West had been a mean son of a gun.
    He had broken every rule in the book, and had gotten away with it.
    He had fought the law, and he had won.
    Until the day Ralph Cutter betrayed him.
    That was the day the law finally won.
    That was the day Nick West died.
    Until now.
    I'm comin' for you, Nick. Watch your back.

Different From New York

Thunder Mountain, Colorado
December 12, 1880

Agnes stood on the footbridge, staring down at the crystal blue stream.
    Although it was nearly dark, she could just make out her reflection in the water.
    Shivering, Agnes took a deep breath of the fresh mountain air. She looked up at the night sky with the full moon and twinkling stars peering down at her.
    Thunder Mountain, Colorado was very different from New York.
    A single tear slid down her round cheek. She quickly wiped it away.

Sleeping In The Church

Just after ten of the clock that night

Despite the late hour, Nathaniel returned to the church to retrieve his bible and notes.

Making his way up the aisle, he suddenly came to the realization he was not alone.

Nathaniel silently stood in the center of the room.

Moments later, a shadowed figure sat up in the front pew.

"May I help you?" His voice softly echoed throughout the church.

The shadowed figure quickly stood. Although dark, Nathaniel realized the trespasser was a woman.

A very unkempt, dark-haired woman.

So as not to frighten her, Nathaniel slowly made his way toward her. Again, he asked, "May I help you?"

"Are you the minister of this church?"

Smiling, he replied, "I am."

The young woman looked down at the floor for a moment. Then, looking back up at him, she asked, "Is the Sunday school teacher position still available?"

Trying to get a good look at her in the darkness, Nathaniel asked, "Who are you?"

She was silent for a moment before saying, "Agnes Crandall."

"Why are you sleeping in the church, Miss Crandall?"

"I have no money to stay in the hotel, nor the boardinghouse."

"I cannot allow you to sleep in the church, but I will drive you to the boardinghouse, and take care of the charges for a night. Tomorrow, we will discuss your situation over breakfast in the hotel's dining room."

Defensively, Agnes asked, "Why are you willing to help me?"

"I'm a minister. It's my duty to help those in need."

"I cannot allow you to pay my room and board."

"You can pay me back once you acquire a position."

Agnes remained silent for a moment before quietly saying, "Thank you."

Smiling, Nathaniel said, "My name is Reverend Nathaniel Weston."

"Hearth And Home"

December 13, 1880

The early morning sunlight played across Agnes' face.

Groaning, she slowly opened her eyes, and forced herself to focus on her surroundings.

Although the blue and cream décor reminded her of her

Brooklyn Heights bedchamber, this room had a warm, loving "hearth and home" feel to it.

A knock on the bedroom door startled her.

Agnes quickly sat up, wondering if her parents had found her. Wondering if Rabbi Kuhn had found her.

She got out of bed, and made her way across the carpeted floor to the door.

Her heart beat a little too fast as she unlocked the door, and slowly opened it.

Something To Hide

A blond-haired, spectacled woman, pulling a small trunk, pushed past Agnes, and entered the room.

"I am lending you some things until you are able to purchase your own. Feel free to make the necessary alterations. I didn't take your height, or your measurements, into account."

"Who are you?"

Smiling sheepishly, the woman offered her hand. "I should have introduced myself before I started talking a mile a minute. I am Callie Cooper, Thunder Mountain's newspaper reporter." Proudly, she continued, "Not to mention town gossip."

Agnes shook her offered hand. "How did you know I needed these things?"

"Reverend Weston told me."

Agnes didn't know why she felt a small pang of jealousy. "Thank you for your generosity, Miss Cooper."

"Please call me Callie, Miss Crandall."

"Please call me Agnes."

Although she had not been granted permission to do so, Callie sat down in the white wicker chair by the matching escritoire. "You have a New York accent. What part of New York are you from?"

"Brooklyn."

Callie smiled. "Are you hiding something, Agnes?"

Agnes stared at her for a moment before asking, "Why do you ask?"

"Those who come to Thunder Mountain, Colorado have something to hide."

"Do you have something to hide, Callie?"

Callie smiled. "Like I said, those who come to Thunder Mountain, Colorado have something to hide." She stood. "It's time for me to return to the newspaper office. Have a good breakfast with Reverend Weston." She left the room, closing the door behind her.

After several long moments, Agnes made her way over to the

escritoire, and opened the drawer. Staring down at the necklace that marked her as a young Jewish woman, she came to the realization that she must say goodbye to her religion.
It would not be hard to do. She hated being Jewish. Being Jewish was nothing but a curse.

AN ANGEL WITH A SECRET

Eleven of the clock that morning

I'm comin' for you, Nick. Watch your back.
Nathaniel had to force himself to forget Ralph Cutter's threat. Taking a sip of tea, his gaze focused on the town's prodigal son, Sheriff Alexander Main.
According to Miss Cooper, though, Main's return had been anything but something to rejoice over.
The sudden appearance of a dark-haired woman caught his gaze. He slowly stood.
Standing in the doorway to the hotel's dining room, wearing an ill-fitted green and cream striped dress under a green coat, was a uniquely beautiful, dark-haired angel.
Miss Agnes Crandall.
An angel with a secret.

CHAPTER THREE

INTERVIEW

Reverend Nathaniel Weston was not a handsome man.

He was ruggedly handsome.

Agnes' dark eyes widened. Was she going to go to hell for thinking such thoughts about a man of God?

She quickly took a sip of hot tea.

"Tell me, Miss Crandall, how was it you came to Thunder Mountain without a cent to your name?" Nathaniel asked. "Not to mention no luggage?"

Agnes took another sip of hot tea, and then placed the cup on the saucer. "One does not think about money, not to mention luggage, after a train accident."

"Are your references with your luggage and money, Miss Crandall?

Grimacing, Agnes said, "Unfortunately, yes."

Nathaniel stared at her for a moment before saying, "Give me the names of your contacts, and I will send them a telegram."

Agnes thought quickly, and then said, "I just proved to you I will not make a good Sunday school teacher, Reverend Weston. I lied. I do not have any references because I am not a Sunday school teacher. I saw the advertisement for the position in the newspaper, and suddenly found myself on the next train here."

Gently, Nathaniel asked, "Was there a train accident?"

Agnes shook her dark head.

Although he knew she was telling the truth, there were still holes in her story.

Just as he was about to tell her the position was hers, she quickly stood. "When I find an available position, I will pay you back." She hurried out of the dining room.

NEW SHERIFF?

I'm comin' for you, Nick. Watch your back.

"Interesting telegram, Reverend Weston?"

Nathaniel quickly pocketed the threat, and looked up at the sheriff. "Just another boring telegram regarding supplies I ordered."

Sheriff Main stared at him for a moment before asking, "Is there something I need to know, Weston?"

"Are you going to be our new sheriff?"

Knowing that Reverend Weston had deliberately changed the subject, Sheriff Main smiled. "I still haven't decided. After all, who'd want to return to a town that doesn't forget or forgive?"

A Talk Between Two Outlaws

"I need to talk with you."

Edith waited until Jenny left the room before asking, "What's wrong, Nathaniel?"

Nathaniel handed her the threatening telegram. While she read it, he paced the parlor floor.

Edith remained silent, pondering her thoughts for a moment. "I know the truth about you. I know that you're an outlaw."

Nathaniel frowned. "Did Zachary tell you?"

Defensively, Edith said, "Zachary is a very trustworthy man. He would never tell another's confidence!" Smiling sheepishly, she continued, "Being an outlaw myself, I have no trouble smelling another outlaw a mile away."

Nathaniel sat down in one of the chairs with a sigh.

Edith stared at him for a moment before asking, "Why are you telling me your secret, Nathaniel? Do you think I can help in any way?"

"I need to talk to someone who has been in my boots. Someone who has fought the law. And won."

"In case you've forgotten, Nathaniel, my life almost ended at the end of a rope." Staring down at the telegram, she asked, "What did you do to piss this dude off?"

"I really didn't do anything to piss Ralph Cutter off. I just told him I didn't trust him. I don't know what the bigger mistake was; trusting him, or not trusting him."

Edith's baby blue eyes widened. "Did you say Ralph Cutter?"

"Yes." Nathaniel frowned. "Why?" His eyes widened. "Do you know him?"

Edith groaned. "Let's just say I regret that my aim was off."

Nathaniel arched one brow. "I think this calls for a stiff drink."

"Make mine a double. A double shot of water."

The Cooking Position

Miss Mabel entered the kitchen where Agnes stood at the sink, washing the supper dishes. "Miss Crandall, everyone is still raving about tonight's supper."

Modestly, Agnes quietly said, "It was nothing."

"It wasn't nothing, Miss Crandall. It was something. It's no secret my cooking is terrible. Thanks to Miss Cooper, I eat my terrible cooking alone."

For the first time in a long time, Agnes smiled.

Miss Mabel stared at her for a moment before asking, "Are you still in need of a position?"

"Yes," Agnes quietly said.

"How would you like to be my cook? Although you will be getting your room and board for free, I will still pay you ten dollars a week."

"That is a very generous offer."

"Will you accept the position, Miss Crandall?"

Agnes stared down at the plate she was washing. After several long moments, she nodded. "Yes."

The Sunday School Teacher Position

December 18, 1880

Nathaniel entered *Thunder Mountain General Store* to buy canned vegetables for supper.

While Gertrude Wilson turned her back on him, a cheerful Albert Wilson asked, "How was Zachary and Edith's wedding, Reverend Weston?"

Looking at Mrs. Wilson, Nathaniel said, "The wedding was beautiful. Thank you for asking, Mr. Wilson."

Just then, Miss Crandall came to the counter with her purchases. "Put these on my account, please."

Nathaniel peered at her for a moment before asking, "How is your position at the boardinghouse, Miss Crandall?"

"I never enjoyed cooking until now. The only challenge is seeing to everyone's likes and dislikes."

"Miss Crandall, are you still interested in the Sunday school teacher position?"

He did not miss the sudden look of happiness on her face.

"Yes," she whispered.

He smiled. "I will pay you five dollars every Sunday. Is that fair?"

"That is very fair. Thank you." And then, wrinkling her brow, she asked, "Why did you give me the position, Reverend Weston?"

"I believe in giving people a chance." He paused a moment before continuing, "As long as they're deserving of it."

Questioning Agnes

Nathaniel exited the store just as Sheriff Main ascended the first step.

"I need to ask you a question, Sheriff Main."

"What is it, Reverend?"

"Where did Miss Crandall get on your train?"

Without hesitation, Sheriff Main said, "In Boston. Why?"

"Did she have a ticket?"

"No. She told the conductor and me she had been in a train accident. I paid for her trip."

"Did you believe her?"

"No." He looked at the minister for a moment before asking, "Why are you questioning her?"

"I just hired her to be the new Sunday school teacher."

"Why would you hire her if you don't know anything about her?"

"We all have secrets. And unless one is totally bad to the bone, we all deserve a second chance."

CHAPTER FOUR

THE MORNING AFTER

December 19, 1880

Edith Scalen slowly awoke to her husband's sensual caresses.
"Did I wake you?" he gently whispered.
"You know damn well you did."
Zachary smiled. "Would you like me to stop?"
"You know damn well I don't." Touching his face gently, she brought her mouth to his, and kissed him with hard, hot passion.

A THUNDER MOUNTAIN, COLORADO SNOWFALL

Smiling, Edith said, "I'm finally experiencing a Thunder Mountain, Colorado snowfall."
Zachary enfolded his wife in his arms as she stared out the bedroom window. In the distance, a spectacular view of Thunder Mountain greeted them.
"This magnificence will greet you every morning," Zachary said, his voice low and seductive.
Edith reached behind her, and wrapped her small hand around his large cock. For the first time in his life, he blushed. "I meant the view outside our window."
Edith smiled a very naughty smile. "I know."

LITTLE WOMEN

Zachary awoke to find his wife reading a worn copy of *Little Women*. Slightly groggy, he said, "Beth dies."
Edith playfully smacked him with her book. "And how would you know Beth dies?"
Nonchalantly, Zachary said, "I read the book."
Raising one perfectly arched dark brow, Edith asked, "You read *Little Women?*"

"Don't act so surprised. I have two younger sisters."

"You- You have two younger sisters? What else haven't you told me?"

Zachary took her in his arms. "Edith, there will be plenty of time to talk about us. We are on our honeymoon. Making love is all that matters."

Edith laughed. She gently caressed his face, and then said, "I'm going to read *Little Women* with Jenny. I'm going to read all the classics with her. And, I want to school her at home."

Zachary lovingly smiled. "I want you to school Jenny at home. I will not allow her to be taught by someone who gets pleasure out of punishing children." He was silent for a moment before saying, "Now, open the book, and read the part where Jo and Professor Bhaer meet for the first time."

Once again, she raised one perfectly arched dark brow.

"Don't act so surprised I know the book by heart."

Edith smiled. "What else haven't you told me?"

Zachary whispered in her ear.

Her eyes widened in surprise.

Attending Church

When Agnes entered the parlor, Nathaniel placed his cup and saucer on the coffee table, and stood.

"Hello, Reverend Weston. Miss Mabel said you wanted to speak with me."

"Why weren't you in church this morning, Miss Crandall?"

"I had to finish preparing the noon meal. And now, I'm putting the finishing touches on supper. Is there a problem?"

"As the Sunday school teacher, it is your duty to attend church."

"I did not realize I was expected to attend church." She frowned. Although she barely knew him, she knew the minister was not himself this day. Smiling, she continued, "Would you care to stay for supper?"

"No, thank you. Good afternoon." He exited the parlor.

Agnes knew something was very wrong.

Intrigued, she returned to the kitchen.

In Danger

Lost in his thoughts, Nathaniel did not realize he was in danger until he hit the ground.

When a hard body landed on top of him, his eyes rolled back into his head, and he lost consciousness.

CHAPTER FIVE

AMBUSHED BY AN INDIAN

"Nick? Nick?"

Nathaniel groaned, and slowly opened his eyes. His gaze focused on the man above him.

"Damien?"

"You need to be more aware of your surroundings, Nick," Damien Midnight Storm said.

Nathaniel sheepishly grinned. "I didn't expect to be ambushed by an Indian."

"Thunder Mountain, Colorado is not immune to Indian attacks, Nick. Would you like me to help you up?"

Nathaniel glared at his friend. "No, thank you. I plan on lying here all night."

Damien carefully helped him to stand. They stared at each other for a moment, and then hugged.

"It's been two long years," Nathaniel said. "Are you still looking for your mother and sister?"

Damien looked down at the snow-covered ground. Quietly, he said, "I found them."

Nathaniel knew not to press his friend for details. Damien would talk when he was ready.

"I would like a word with you, Reverend Weston!"

"Jesus Christ!" Nathaniel swore under his breath.

Damien arched one raven brow. "Since when do ministers take the Lord's name in vain?"

"When confronted by a Main, Jesus himself would take the Lord's name in vain," Nathaniel quipped.

Quickly crossing the street, Marjorie Main came up to them. Ignoring the Indian, she gave the minister a glaring look. "How could you?"

Amused, Nathaniel asked, "Would you care to elaborate, Miss Main?"

Marjorie did not return his amusement. "How could you marry an outlaw?"

When Damien arched his brow again, Nathaniel explained, "I married an outlaw to a man."

Marjorie stamped her foot. "Are you listening to me, Reverend Weston?"

"The entire town, including Boot Hill, is listening, Miss Main," Nathaniel said.

At the mention of Boot Hill, Marjorie, in a low, cold voice, said, "Maggie Lawton murdered my brother. I will see to it your credentials are revoked for daring to marry her in God's house!" She quickly stormed away.

Damien remained silent for a moment. "You sure have a way with the ladies, Nick."

"She's usually as serious and quiet as a church mouse. She's the librarian."

"Very interesting," Damien drawled, watching as the librarian hurried down the street.

"Would you care to join me for supper?" Nathaniel asked. "There is much to discuss."

"I would be honored, old friend," Damien said.

"By the way, my name is Nathaniel. Do not call me Nick." Staring down at the ground, he quietly said, "Nick is dead."

SUICIDAL

Damien pushed his empty plate away, and leaned back in his chair. "You've outdone yourself, Ni- Nathaniel."

Nathaniel shrugged. "It was nothing."

"Don't be modest. You're a great cook."

Nathaniel removed the plates from the table, and carried them to the sink. While he filled two cups with hot coffee, Damien watched him for a moment. "When are you going to start looking for a wife?"

Not looking at his friend, Nathaniel said, "I'm not the marrying kind."

"You are a respectable minister, Nathaniel. You have paid your dues."

"When Thunder Mountain learns my secret, I will no longer be respectable. No woman will want to marry me."

Damien frowned. "How would this town learn your secret?"

Nathaniel took the telegram from his pocket, and handed it to his friend.

Damien read it, and swore under his breath. "When?" he quietly asked.

"I don't know."

"What is your plan?"

Nathaniel did not answer him.

Damien stared incredulously at him for a moment. "You don't have a plan? Are you stupid?"

"More like suicidal."

"What?"

"I'm going to let Ralph Cutter kill me."

Damien quickly stood, knocking over his chair. "I should scalp you for daring to suggest such a thing!"

"I escaped from prison, Damien. When the law finds me, I will hang. That's why I plan to let Ralph Cutter come after me, and kill me."

"As your friend, I will not let that happen. When this is all over, Ralph Cutter will be the one who pays. Not you!"

"The law won't see it your way."

"When I'm through with them, the law will see who the true villain is."

Nathaniel looked at him for a moment. "I still don't understand why you're my friend."

"You aren't the cold, hard outlaw you pretend to be, Nathaniel. You have a heart. And you have a soul."

Nathaniel swallowed, and quickly turned away from his friend. Taking a dish from the hot, soapy water in the sink, he began to wash it.

Wisely changing the subject, Damien said, "Tell me more about the intriguing Miss Marjorie Main."

That Went Well.

"You're awfully quiet this evening," Zachary said, taking a bite of potato.

Edith placed her knife and fork on her plate, and looked at her husband. "I know about Ralph Cutter's threats."

Zachary paused for a moment before placing his utensils on his plate. "How?"

"Nathaniel told me."

"I wish he hadn't."

"Why would you say that?"

"As your husband, it is my duty to protect you from danger."

Edith glared at him. "I do not need a man's protection!" She quickly stood, and stormed out of the dining room.

Zachary remained seated. After several long moments, he said, out loud, "That went well." He went back to his supper.

Sorry

"I'm sorry."

Zachary looked up from his paperwork. His wife stood in the doorway to his study, dressed for bed.

Edith entered the room, and went to her husband. She looked at him for a moment before straddling his lap.

"Does this mean I won't be sleeping in the bathtub?"

Edith smiled. "In my profession, I could not allow myself to be dependent on a man. It will take time before I can depend on you."

"You are brave, strong, and tough. You can take care of yourself. I just want to protect you, and keep you safe. I love you."

Edith smiled, and wiped at a tear that threatened to fall. "I'm sorry," she whispered.

Zachary gently stroked her round cheek. "You don't have to be sorry, Sweetheart. You didn't do anything wrong." He was quiet for a moment before continuing, "Tell me about Ralph Cutter, and don't leave anything out."

Unfinished Business

Calico, Kansas
December 26, 1880

Holding a wet newspaper in his hand, Ralph Cutter entered the sheriff's office.

"I am going to Thunder Mountain, Colorado, Boss."

Sheriff Bill Anderson leaned back in his chair, and stared up at his foreman. "What for?"

"I have unfinished business."

"With Maggie Lawton?"

"She is on my list."

"Who is at the top of your list?"

"Nick West."

"Nick West. Once an outlaw, now a preacher. Thunder Mountain, Colorado is an exciting place to live these days, isn't it?"

"Nick West will regret the day he betrayed me!"

"Have a safe trip, Ralph. Don't forget to say hello to Caroline for me."

CHAPTER SIX

ADVISEMENT

Thunder Mountain, Colorado
December 26, 1880

When Agnes entered the parlor, Nathaniel placed his cup and saucer on the coffee table, and stood.
"What did I do wrong this time, Reverend Weston?"
Nathaniel smiled. "You didn't do anything wrong, Miss Crandall. I came here to apologize."
Agnes smiled tightly. "Thank you."
"What do you have against going to church?"
"I don't have anything against going to church."
"You don't want to be there."
"I thought you were here to apologize. Instead, you're judging me."
"I don't judge, Miss Crandall. I only advise."
"If I want your advisement, I'll ask for it! I will continue coming to church because it is expected of me. Good day, Reverend Weston." She turned, and left the parlor.
Nathaniel stood where he was for several long moments. And then, he grinned. The fiery and stubborn Miss Crandall would keep him from thinking about Ralph Cutter.
And dying.

TRUST

December 27, 1880-Just after midnight

Callie entered the kitchen to find Agnes drinking a cup of hot tea.
"Having a midnight snack?"
"I couldn't sleep," Agnes said. "Are you having trouble sleeping, too?"
Callie sat down at the table, and took a green apple from the

bowl. She took a bite, chewed, and swallowed. "I don't sleep."

"You don't sleep? Why not?"

"I don't like sleeping. Besides, there's too much work to be done. It's easier to do when there's no one around to bother me." She took another bite of apple, and stared down at the wooden table.

Agnes was not fooled. Callie's dark circles were very noticeable, and Agnes suspected she was hiding something.

"You're a good writer, Callie."

Arching one dark gold brow, Callie stared at Agnes for a moment before saying, "Either you're lying, or I'm dreaming."

Agnes laughed. "Neither. You do and say what you want, damn the consequences."

"You'll think differently when your secrets are featured in my newspaper."

"Are you going to reveal my secrets?"

Callie smiled. "Do you have any?"

Agnes stared at her for a moment before asking, "Why do you report secrets and gossip?"

"Secrets and gossip sell newspapers. I thought you said I was a good writer."

"You are a good writer, Callie. What you are not is a good friend."

"I thought you admired me for doing and saying what I want, damn the consequences."

"I would admire you even more if you didn't hurt people with your words. A person should be able to trust a friend with their confidences." Standing, she took her cup to the sink. Turning back, she said, "Until I can trust you with my confidences, Miss Cooper, stay away from me!" She hurried up the back staircase.

Callie just sat there for a moment longer before placing her apple on the table.

She swallowed.

SISTERS

December 28, 1880

"I want sisters, Mother."

Edith looked at Jenny. "You do? What about brothers?"

Jenny shook her dark head. "I want sisters. Three."

Edith looked down at the book in her lap. "Who is your favorite sister?"

"Beth. Who is your favorite sister?"

"My favorite is Jo."

Edith glanced up, and noticed Hannah Porter standing in the doorway, smiling. Edith stood, went to the other woman, and warmly greeted her.

"I apologize for disturbing your lesson," Hannah said.

"Don't apologize, Hannah. Jenny and I are reading *Little Women.*"

"*Little Women* is one of my favorite books."

After Jenny left the room, Edith rang for tea and scones, and then invited the other woman to sit down on the sofa with her.

Hannah remained silent for a moment before saying, "I do not want Carl to attend a school that relishes in corporal punishment. Would you be willing to teach him?" Not giving Edith a chance to answer, she continued, "I'll understand if you say no, Edith."

"Why would I say no, Hannah? I'm honored you would ask. Just out of curiosity, why can't you teach him?"

"I want him to be taught by an educated teacher." Hannah looked down at her lap, and smiled. Softly, she said, "I won't have time to properly teach him once the baby is born."

Edith smiled. "Hannah, I'm so happy for you! Congratulations!" She hugged her friend.

"We'll be having our babies around the same time."

Edith wrinkled her dark brow in confusion. "What?"

"You may not realize it, but you are expecting. You have a glow that only expectant women have."

Edith placed her small hand on her flat stomach. A baby. She was going to have a baby.

It was several long moments before she finally smiled with happiness.

ONCE AN OUTLAW, ALWAYS AN OUTLAW

Zachary stood when Nathaniel entered his office, and warmly greeted his friend. "Would you care for a brandy?"

"Since it's after five, and I'm going home afterward, a brandy would be great. Thank you."

After several moments of small talk, Zachary got straight to the point. "Why did you tell Edith about your situation?"

"I needed to talk with another outlaw."

"Ex-outlaw," Zachary said.

"Once an outlaw, always an outlaw."

"That is not true, Nathaniel! The two of you have paid the price. It's time to put your pasts to rest."

Nathaniel stared at Zachary for a moment before saying, "If I'm not mistaken, you would like to forget the fact that Edith is an outlaw."

"If I did, I wouldn't have married her. I just don't want her dwelling on her past."

"No matter how hard one tries, Zachary, one does not forget his or her past."

"Haven't you tried to forget yours, Nathaniel?"

"I will never forget my past. I'm just keeping it a secret from this town."

"When Ralph Cutter comes riding into town, all will be revealed."

Nathaniel was silent for a moment before saying, "Not if I can help it."

Zachary narrowed his black eyes. "Don't do what I think you're going to do, Nathaniel!"

Nathaniel smiled a sad smile. "Don't forget our business agreement, Zachary."

Leaving Town

"I'm leaving town."

Edith stared incredulously at her friend for a moment. "What?"

Callie looked down at her lap, and quietly said, "I do not like who I've become."

"Leaving town is not the answer. If you don't like who you've become, you need to change. No more gossip."

"What Miss Crandall said to me is not the only reason why I'm leaving town."

Edith took her friend's hands in hers. "Callie, if you leave Thunder Mountain, you will not be safe. No one will be able to protect you from your husband, because no one will know you."

"What's going on?"

Edith and Callie looked up to see Zachary standing in the doorway of the parlor. Edith stood, went to her husband, and greeted him with a kiss.

Putting his arm around his wife, he smiled at Callie. "Hello, Callie."

Callie stood, and smiled a strained smile. "Hello, Zachary." Glancing at Edith, she said, "I'll speak with you later." She exited the parlor.

Zachary led his wife to the sofa. "What's wrong with Callie?"

"She got her feelings hurt when Miss Crandall put her in her place."

"Callie does not take unkind words to heart. Is this about

Sheriff Anderson?"

Edith nodded. Sitting, she said, "Callie wants to leave town. I told her she won't be safe if she leaves."

"While I don't want Callie to leave, it is her decision."

"I wonder if Sheriff Anderson saw the wedding photograph in the newspaper."

There was no doubt in Zachary's mind that the sheriff had seen it. And there was definitely no doubt in Zachary's mind that the sheriff was plotting revenge against his wife. Although Zachary was a lover of all things Wild West, he did not like the danger of revenge. And he most definitely did not like the fact that Edith would be a part of this dangerous revenge.

Nathaniel had been wrong when he said, "Once an outlaw, always an outlaw."

When Sheriff Anderson and Ralph Cutter came riding into town, he would make damn well sure his wife was nowhere in sight!

And he would most definitely make damn well sure his wife put her outlaw past behind her!

Forever!

CHAPTER SEVEN

Defending A Friend

December 29, 1880

"You are not welcome here, Mrs. Scalen!"

"I am here to see Miss Crandall, Miss Mabel."

Miss Mabel stared at the outlaw for a moment before allowing her to enter the boardinghouse.

Edith entered the kitchen, where Miss Crandall was cooking supper. Despite the fact that she was angry at the other woman, her mouth watered at the sight and smell of the feast fit for a king.

Chopping onions, Agnes asked, "Does the reason for your visit concern Miss Cooper?"

"Miss Crandall, you are new to this town. It's not wise to make enemies during your first few weeks."

Agnes glanced at the other woman, and said, "I don't take advice from an outlaw."

"I didn't come here to offer advice. I came here to tell you that Miss Cooper is my friend."

"Miss Cooper only cares about making money."

"Money is important," Edith said.

"Love is more important," Agnes countered.

Edith stared at the other woman for a moment before asking, "Did you make all of this food by yourself? It looks, and smells, delicious."

Agnes found herself smiling. "Thank you."

Suddenly, Edith's eyes widened. Covering her mouth with one gloved hand, she hurried to the back door, quickly opened it, and ran outside.

To the empty kitchen, Agnes asked, "Was it something that I said? Or cooked?" Shrugging, she returned to the supper preparations.

Cowboy Dave

December 31, 1880-Half past five of the clock in the afternoon

As twilight descended upon the town, the New Year's Eve festivities began.

"Cowboy Dave" Nelson rode into town, and tethered his horse, Barney, to a hitching post. He moseyed up Main Street, greeting friends, and making single ladies, not to mention saloon girls, swoon.

Serving baked beans to a hungry festivity-goer, Miss Mabel paused, and watched as Cowboy Dave shared some hearty laughs with Mr. Scalen and Mr. Lord.

Beside her, Agnes asked, "Who's the cowboy?"

"That's Cowboy Dave," Hannah Porter said, answering for Miss Mabel. "The Nelson ranch is the largest, and the most coveted, spread in the territory."

Slightly worried, Agnes asked, "Have there been any problems?"

"Not yet, thank God," Miss Mabel answered.

Cowboy Dave came to the serving table, and said, "Howdy, ladies." He looked at Miss Mabel, and grinned. "Howdy, Miss Mabel."

"Good evening, Mr. Nelson," Miss Mabel replied.

"I'm looking forward to tasting your baked beans."

"Miss Crandall made them," Miss Mabel said.

"Would you be so kind as to give me a taste of Miss Agnes' baked beans, Miss Mabel?"

Miss Mabel spooned a very tiny amount of baked beans onto Cowboy Dave's plate. He glanced at the beans, and then looked at her. Smiling, he said, "You really know how to charm the socks right off a snake, Miss Mabel. Make sure to save a dance for me." Winking, he walked away.

"He sure is charming," Agnes said.

Miss Mabel's lips compressed into a thin line as she watched two saloon girls cozy up to the cowboy.

Thunder Mountain Square Dance

Standing on top of an overturned apple crate, Nathaniel shouted, "Gentlemen, grab your partners! It's time to Thunder Mountain Square Dance!"

Hunter Lord walked over to where Rose and several girls stood, and asked, "Would you care to dance, Rose?"

Rose shook her head.

One of the girls said, "I'll dance with you, Hunter."

They quickly hurried over to the dirt dance floor.

Cowboy Dave sauntered over to Miss Mabel, who was heavily involved in a quilting project with several elderly ladies. "Would you care to dance, Miss Mabel?"

Miss Mabel shook her head.

One of the elderly ladies stood, and said, "I'll dance with you, Cowboy Dave."

He looked at the old woman for a moment before escorting her to the dirt dance floor.

When the dancers took their places, Nathaniel shouted, "Fiddle and banjo, let the music begin!"

As the dance began, onlookers clapped their hands together, and tapped their feet in time to the music.

From his position on top of the apple crate, Nathaniel watched as Miss Crandall danced with Zachary. He felt envy toward his friend. He wanted to be the man dancing with Miss Crandall.

With Agnes.

As the music came to a rollicking crescendo, everyone clapped. Zachary returned to his wife's side, while Agnes made her way over to Nathaniel. He looked at her, and smiled. She returned his smile.

"Would you like some pie, Reverend Weston?"

I want you, he thought.

REFUSING PUNCH TO A PROSTITUTE

"I would like a cup of punch, please."

"We do not serve prostitutes."

It was several long moments before Rose could finally speak. "What did you say?"

"You heard me," Viola Main said sternly.

Glaring at the older woman, Rose said, "And you heard me! I would like a cup of punch."

Marjorie, Hunter, Nathaniel, and Callie made their way to the refreshment table. Marjorie came to stand beside her mother.

Looking at Viola Main, Hunter asked, "What's going on?"

"I have a right to refuse service to prostitutes," Viola Main answered.

Obviously embarrassed by her mother's behavior, Marjorie closed her eyes, and bowed her blond head.

"Give the lady her punch," Hunter quietly ordered.

Viola Main stood there.

"Give the lady her goddamned punch!"

Placing her hand on Hunter's arm, Rose quietly said, "Hunter, please don't do this."

Nathaniel said, "Mrs. Main, please remove yourself from the serving table. Miss Cooper will take your place for the rest of the evening."

"I will not remove myself from the serving table, Reverend Weston!" Viola Main said defensively.

Marjorie gently touched her mother's arm, and quietly said, "Mother, it's time to go home."

Nathaniel was silent for a moment before saying, "I have decided that my sermon on Sunday will be entitled, "We Are All God's Children"." Glaring at Viola Main, he said, "God loves every single one of His children. When you refuse to give a cup of punch to a woman, simply because she's a prostitute, you're refusing Him!"

Tears threatening to spill down her cheeks, Rose, unable to look at Mrs. Main, said, "Since you have refused to give me a cup of punch, Mrs. Main, tell your husband I am refusing to give him a good lay."

You tell her, Rose!" Callie exclaimed.

Everyone turned to look at her. Smiling sheepishly, she took her place behind the serving table.

Unable to keep her tears from falling, Rose quickly hurried away.

BEAUTIFUL SOILED DOVE

Standing in the shadows, Sheriff Alexander Main watched as the beautiful soiled dove ran down Main Street toward the saloon.

SOLITAIRE

Sheriff Alexander Main entered *The Lord Above Saloon.*

Looking up from her game of Solitaire, Rose said, "We're closed."

"Since when is a saloon closed?"

"Since I say so."

Alexander looked at her for a moment. "Are you all right?"

Studying the hand she had dealt, she asked, "Why wouldn't I be all right?"

Alexander couldn't help but smile. "You're not the tough Madame that you pretend to be, Rose."

Rose tossed her cards on the table, and looked up at him. "Go find someone to arrest, Sheriff!"

"I'm not the sheriff."

"Yet." She began a new game of Solitaire.

Alexander watched her play for a moment before leaving the saloon.

Rose played until she couldn't play anymore. She picked up the cards, and stared at them.

And then, she flung them high into the air.

MOONSHINE

"This is some good moonshine, Tater Bob."

"The best," Tater Bob said.

"Why does it taste so good?" Luke asked.

"It's the mountain snow," Tater Bob said.

Suddenly, Luke whispered, "Someone's comin'!"

"They will not get my moonshine!" Tater Bob whispered furiously, putting protective arms around the barrel in front of him.

Nathaniel, Damien, Hunter, and Cowboy Dave entered the barn, and climbed the ladder to the hayloft. Nathaniel looked at Luke, then at Tater Bob. "What are you two doing?"

"We're shearin' sheep!" Tater Bob snapped. "What does it look like we're doin'?"

Nathaniel had to control the urge to laugh. "Moonshine is illegal, Tater Bob. You know that."

"No shit, Dude!" Tater Bob exclaimed.

Nathaniel could not hold back his laughter any longer. He was not alone. Hunter was laughing so hard, his sides hurt, while Cowboy Dave had to hold on to Damien to keep from collapsing into the hay.

When Nathaniel could finally speak, he said, "I will not have you arrested on one condition."

"What condition would that be?" Luke asked.

"Share some of your moonshine with us. After the night I've just had, I am badly in need of a stiff drink."

Luke, Tater Bob, Damien, Hunter, and Cowboy Dave all turned at once to look at him.

And then, once again, everyone burst out laughing.

Nathaniel, Damien, Hunter, and Cowboy Dave gladly accepted several rounds of highly potent moonshine.

"This is some good moonshine, Tater Bob," Nathaniel said.

"The best," Tater Bob agreed.

COUNTING DOWN TO 1881

Ten minutes to midnight

Champagne was being passed around to ring in the New Year.

When Callie offered Hannah Porter a glass, she put her hand

on her flat stomach, and smiled. Josiah Porter lovingly put his arm around his wife.

"Congratulations!" Callie exclaimed. "Do you know when your bundle of joy is due?"

"Early August," Hannah said.

Edith looked up at her husband. She had wanted to wait until they were in bed, but she suddenly realized that the best time to tell him was while they were ringing in 1881. Smiling, she said, "Zachary, Josiah and Hannah are not the only ones who are going to have a baby."

Zachary stared down at his wife for a moment before taking her in his arms, and kissing her.

Amidst the clapping and cheering, Callie and several others finished passing out the champagne.

"It's time!" Callie exclaimed. "Ten...nine...eight..."

As one, the townspeople of Thunder Mountain, Colorado counted down the last seven seconds to midnight.

To Hell With Propriety!

January 1, 1881-Seconds after midnight

Walking back to the boardinghouse, Agnes paused to stare up at the colorful fireworks exploding in the midnight sky. What a spectacular sight! It had never been this spectacular back in New York.

"Miss Crandall?"

Agnes turned to find Reverend Weston walking toward her.

Tripping on the boardwalk, he quickly caught himself to keep from falling.

Agnes' eyes narrowed. "Are you drunk, Reverend Weston?"

Nathaniel sheepishly smiled. "Just a little moonshine."

"Moonshine?" She wrinkled her brow in confusion. "Isn't that illegal?"

"I won't tell if you won't tell."

Rolling her dark eyes, Agnes said, "I will have someone take you home."

"I want you to take me home."

Agnes swallowed. "Reverend Weston, it will not be proper for me to take you home."

"To hell with propriety!"

"Reverend Weston!"

Nathaniel closed the distance between them, and took her in his arms. Before she could blink, and breathe, he lowered his head.

And kissed her.

Last Kiss

Minutes after midnight

Ralph Cutter stood in the shadows, and watched as Nick West kissed a tall, dark-haired woman. He smiled, and softly said, "Enjoy your kiss, Nick. After all, it's goin' to be your last."

CHAPTER EIGHT

The Kiss

Eight of the clock that morning

Agnes stared up at the ceiling.

Having spent a sleepless night thinking about the kiss, she was exhausted.

Why had she allowed Reverend Weston to kiss her?

Why had she allowed herself to kiss him back?

Groaning, Agnes rolled over, and buried herself under the warm bedclothes.

How would she be able to face him?

Oh, God.

No Time!

Brooklyn Heights, Brooklyn, New York
January 2, 1881

"Where on earth is she?"

Rivkah Berezovsky watched as Rabbi Kuhn paced the parlor floor. She wrinkled her red brow in confusion. There was something about him she could not put her finger on. Something about him that made her feel uneasy. She looked at her husband. His face was emotionless.

"I have paid top dollar for private detectives who don't know how to do their job!" Rabbi Kuhn continued.

"Rachel will send word eventually," Rivkah Berezovsky said.

"There is no time!" Rabbi Kuhn exclaimed.

Rabbi Viktor Berezovsky looked at his wife. He then looked back at the young rabbi, and asked, "What do you mean by that, Jacob?"

Rabbi Kuhn was silent for a moment before saying, "We cannot waste any more time. We need to find Rachel. Now!"

REASONS

Thunder Mountain, Colorado
January 2, 1881-Nine of the clock that morning

Agnes took a deep breath, entered the empty church, and made her way down the aisle toward Reverend Weston.
Placing a bible on a pew, Nathaniel warmly smiled at her. "What are you doing here this early, Miss Crandall? You don't have to be here for another hour."
"I wanted to speak with you, Reverend Weston."
Nathaniel's smile disappeared. "No doubt about our kiss."
"Why did you kiss me?"
"I apologize for having kissed you, Miss Crandall. I was drunk."
"Being drunk was not the reason why you kissed me. You kissed me because you wanted to kiss me. The moonshine just helped you do it."
Nathaniel smiled. "You weren't drunk. What was your reason for kissing me back, Miss Crandall?"
Agnes just stared at him for a moment before exclaiming, "I do not have to explain my reason for kissing you back!"
Nathaniel's smile widened. "I'm not drunk now."
It took Agnes a moment to realize the meaning of his statement. "You are no man of God, Reverend Weston! You are the devil incarnate!"
Laughing, Nathaniel said, "I've been called worse."
Glaring at him for a moment, Agnes turned, and stormed up the aisle.
Continuing to laugh, Nathaniel called out after her, "See you in an hour, Miss Crandall!"

I AM A JEW.

January 3, 1881

Agnes had a strong feeling that she was being watched.
Glancing around for a moment, she climbed the wooden steps, and entered *Thunder Mountain General Store*. While Mrs. Wilson ignored her, Mr. Wilson warmly greeted her.
As Agnes made her way toward the back of the store to purchase several bags of flour, an elderly foreign couple entered the store, and asked for a dozen fresh eggs. Agnes heard Mrs. Wilson say, "We don't serve Armenians."

"Gertrude!" her shocked husband warned.

A sudden rush of fury enveloped Agnes. Storming out to the front of the store, she exclaimed, "How dare you turn these people away because they're Armenian, Mrs. Wilson?"

"As the owner of this store, I can choose who I serve, and who I don't serve!"

"You cannot refuse service to someone because of religion or race!"

"Miss Crandall is right, Gertrude," Mr. Wilson said. "Mr. and Mrs. Jebejian are welcome here any time."

"You are making a big mistake, Albert! If we allow foreigners to shop in our store, we will lose business!"

Agnes said, "If you don't allow Mr. and Mrs. Jebejian to shop in your store, Mrs. Wilson, then you will lose Miss Mabel's business. If that happens, then Miss Mabel will not be able to feed her boarders."

Miss Crandall's threat and Mr. Wilson's angry glare did not dissuade Mrs. Wilson from her bigoted tune.

Agnes continued, "By condemning Mr. and Mrs. Jebejian, you condemn me."

Mr. and Mrs. Wilson and Mr. and Mrs. Jebejian stared at her in confusion.

Taking a deep breath, Agnes said, "I am a Jew."

With that profound statement, she left the store, her dark head held high.

CHAPTER NINE

GOD DIDN'T MAKE MISTAKES

Despite the cold, snowy day, Agnes sat in the park, and stared up at the clear, blue sky. Watching a black bird fly gracefully through the air, she wished she could be that bird.

But God had made her a human being.

A female human being.

A Jewish female human being.

Agnes knew she had risked everything by revealing the truth about her religion. There was no doubt that come nightfall, the entire town would know her secret.

How would the residents of Thunder Mountain react to the fact that she was Jewish?

More importantly, how would Reverend Weston react to the fact that she was Jewish?

All her life, Agnes had rebelled against being Jewish. She had hated the prejudice and the attacks. She had hated the severity of it.

On this very day, she came to the sudden realization that she was proud of her religion.

Although Mrs. Wilson's words had hurt, Agnes had stood up for Mr. and Mrs. Jebejian.

She had stood up for herself.

She was no longer ashamed of being Jewish.

Being ashamed meant being against God. God had made her a human being. A female human being. A Jewish female human being.

God didn't make mistakes.

CONSENSUS

Eight of the clock that evening

Agnes stepped up onto the porch of Miss Mabel's Boardinghouse to find Edith Scalen sitting on the porch swing. Without having to ask, Agnes knew why the other woman was there. "What's the consensus?"

Edith stood. "Only a select few want to run you out of town." She paused before continuing, "Miss Mabel is one of them."

Tears gathering in her dark eyes, Agnes looked away. After several long moments, she asked, "What about Reverend Weston?"

"You can ask him yourself."

At the sound of Reverend Weston's voice, Agnes slowly turned, and looked at him. She swallowed.

"Why didn't you tell me you are Jewish?"

"Would it have mattered?"

Nathaniel stared at her for a moment before asking, "Are you ashamed of being Jewish?"

"Not anymore," she quietly said.

Before Nathaniel could say another word, Zachary, carrying a valise, exited the house. Smiling warmly at Agnes, he said, "You will be staying with us tonight, Miss Crandall."

Edith put her arm around Agnes, and led her to the buggy.

Once she was situated in the vehicle, Agnes glanced at Reverend Weston.

What was he thinking?

Oh, God.

A Friend In Miss Cooper

January 4, 1881

An exhausted Agnes entered the dining room to find Edith reading an article in the newspaper to Zachary, who was eating breakfast. There was no doubt in Agnes' mind that the article was about her.

Furious, she grabbed the newspaper, and exclaimed, "Miss Cooper had no right to write about me!"

Edith glanced at her husband for a moment before looking up at Agnes, and saying, "Read the article, Agnes. You'll find that it focuses more on small-town mentality than it does on you. Callie is on your side."

Agnes sat down, and closed her eyes. "I'm beginning to regret what I did."

"Why?" Edith asked. "You stood up to Mrs. Wilson. That meant everything to Mr. and Mrs. Jebejian."

"I no longer have a job, nor do I have a roof over my head," Agnes said.

"You might not have a job, but you have a place with us, for as long as you want it," Zachary said.

"You can help me teach," Edith said. Laughing, she continued, "Timmy Rogers and Nell Pringle will also be joining my very small class."

Agnes did not miss the look Zachary gave Edith. Wondering what that was about, she smiled, and quietly said, "Thank you." She then opened the newspaper, and read the article Miss Cooper had written about the incident. When she finished reading the article, she realized one thing.

She had a friend in Miss Cooper.

PROPOSAL

"I hope I haven't interrupted your supper," Nathaniel said.

"Not at all," Edith said. "You're just in time for dessert."

Following Edith into the parlor, he was warmly greeted by Zachary.

Miss Crandall slowly stood, but did not move forward to greet him. He did not blame her. She had no idea what he was thinking about the incident. About her.

She was in for a big shock.

Nathaniel took a seat on the sofa beside her, and gladly accepted a piece of her lemon cake. After several bites of the delicious dessert, he placed his plate on the coffee table, and turned to face her. "Miss Crandall, will you marry me?"

CHAPTER TEN

Because I Want You.

After practically choking to death on her hot tea, Agnes looked at Reverend Weston, and asked, "Are you drunk again?"

While Edith wrinkled her dark brow in confusion, Zachary burst out laughing, and said, "You sure have a way with the ladies, Nathaniel."

Nathaniel sheepishly smiled, and said, "Damien said the exact same thing."

Suddenly serious, Zachary asked, "What is the meaning of this proposal, Nathaniel?"

Nathaniel was silent for a moment before saying, "I would like to speak with Miss Crandall alone."

Zachary and Edith quickly hurried out of the parlor.

Great! Picking up her tea cup, Agnes took a careful sip of her tea, and then asked, "Why did you ask me to marry you, Reverend Weston?"

"I stayed up all night wondering how I could keep you here. Marrying you is the only way."

Placing the tea cup on the saucer on the coffee table, Agnes said, "Don't do me any favors, Reverend Weston!"

"Why are you so defensive, Miss Crandall?"

"I'm Jewish. That's why."

"What does that mean?"

"It means everything, Reverend Weston. I didn't tell you I was Jewish because I knew what the reaction would be."

"You didn't know what my reaction would be."

"What is your reaction?"

"I want to marry you."

"Why?"

"I want to protect you."

Agnes quickly stood. "Is that the only reason why you want to marry me?"

"No."

"Why do you want to marry me, Reverend Weston?"

Nathaniel was silent for a moment before saying, "Because I want you."

On The Train To Marriage

On the train to Denver, Colorado
January 5, 1881

"I should never have agreed to this," Agnes said, staring down at her lap. "I don't need a knight in shining armor. I need to leave."

Nathaniel took her hand in his, and gently squeezed it.

His touch sent shivers of desire shooting up and down her spine.

"Where would you go, Agnes?"

This was the first time he had spoken her first name.

"I don't know," she quietly said.

Gently, he asked, "Who are you, Agnes?"

"I don't want to talk about my past."

"You will have to talk about it eventually."

Hotly, she exclaimed, "You will know everything there is to know about me when I'm ready to tell you!"

Nathaniel removed his hand from hers.

She suddenly felt empty.

And alone.

She turned to stare out the window at the rushing scenery.

Suddenly, she came to the realization that she should have never revealed the truth about her religion.

Being Jewish truly was a curse.

It Will Be A Cold Day In Hell Before I Sleep With You!

Denver, Colorado
Nine of the clock that evening

Agnes nervously took a sip of red wine, and glanced at her husband.

Husband.

But in name only.

"You haven't touched your supper," Nathaniel said.

"I- I'm not hungry," Agnes quietly said.

"Are you all right, Agnes?"

Agnes glared at him. "Why wouldn't I be all right?"

She was scared to death. Although she knew Reverend Weston, Nathaniel, was a very good man, she did not know anything about him.

Sudden thoughts of Rabbi Jacob Kuhn made her shudder.

Frowning, Nathaniel said, "You're not all right, Agnes."

Agnes stared at him for a moment before saying, "This afternoon, I married a man for reasons that have nothing to do with love. You're right, Nathaniel. I'm not all right."

Nathaniel gently smiled. "Where most marriages are concerned, love comes later."

"My parents had an arranged marriage. They still don't love each other."

"This is the first time you've mentioned a little something about yourself."

"I mentioned that because it pertains to this conversation."

Nathaniel leaned back in his chair, and stared at her for a moment before asking, "Why are you so defensive, Agnes? And don't say it's because you're Jewish."

Agnes just smiled, and took another sip of wine.

Nathaniel continued, "While I may not love you, Agnes, I want you. I will show you just how much I want you later tonight."

Agnes' dark eyes widened. "What do you mean?"

Softly, and with evident desire, Nathaniel repeated, "I will show you just how much I want you later tonight. When we're in bed."

Agnes quickly stood, knocking over her chair. Glaring at her husband, in name only, she exclaimed, "It will be a cold day in hell before I sleep with you!"

CHAPTER ELEVEN

Bread Without Butter

Agnes blushed as everyone in the restaurant turned to stare at her.

Amused, Nathaniel said, "I don't think they heard you. Would you like to say that just a little bit louder?"

Glaring at her husband, Agnes exclaimed, "I'm glad you find this amusing, Nathaniel!"

He took a sip of wine. "You have no idea."

Agnes took a crusty roll from the bread basket, and threw it at his head.

Because he was leaning back in his chair, the roll knocked him off balance.

Lying on the carpeted floor, Nathaniel stared up at his wife. "Can you pass the butter?"

Agnes stormed out of the restaurant.

Nathaniel picked the roll up from the floor, and stared at it for a moment before saying, "I guess this means I'll be sleeping in the bathtub tonight." Taking a bite of the roll, he said, "This actually tastes good without butter."

A Bigot

Thunder Mountain, Colorado
Half past nine of the clock that evening

Miss Mabel stepped out onto the porch for a breath of fresh air. To her dismay, Cowboy Dave was sitting on the porch swing.

"What are you doing here, Mr. Nelson? You're-"

"Cowboy Dave."

Ignoring him, she continued, "You're not supposed to be here after nine of the clock."

"It doesn't hurt to break the rules once in awhile, Miss Mabel."

"It is not proper for you to be here, Mr. Nelson!"

"Why don't you like me, Miss Mabel?"

"I don't know what you're talking about."

"You know exactly what I'm talking about. Mabel."

She made her way toward the screen door.

He quickly stood, and blocked her way.

She glared at him for a moment before asking, "Do you really want to know why I don't like you, Mr. Nelson?"

His face was expressionless.

Continuing, she said, "You're a womanizer."

Cowboy Dave grinned. "Is that all?"

"What more do you want?"

"All men like to play with women until they meet the right one."

"You are disgusting, Mr. Nelson!"

"And you are a bigot, Miss Mabel."

Shocked, she exclaimed, "How dare you call me a bigot?"

"You fired Miss Crandall, and threw her out of your boardinghouse because she's Jewish. There's no other name to call you."

"Leave here at once!"

"Not until I do what I came here to do."

Miss Mabel opened her mouth to tell the arrogant cowboy off, but Cowboy Dave took that opportunity to pull her into his arms, and kiss her.

After several long moments, he reluctantly broke the kiss, and hurried down the porch steps. Turning back, he looked up at her with a big grin. "If you claim not to like me, then why did your womanly parts respond to my kiss?" Winking, he moseyed up the street, whistling an improper tune.

Miss Mabel could not move.

Nor could she think.

CALIFORNIA OR ME?

Denver, Colorado
January 6, 1881-Sometime after one of the clock in the morning

The door to the hotel room opened.

Nathaniel slowly sat up, and lay back against the pillows. Although it was completely dark, he knew Agnes was staring at him. After she entered the room, closed the door, and locked it, he asked, "Where have you been?"

"I took a walk."

Nathaniel quickly lit the lamp on the bedside table. He stared at her for several moments before asking, "You walked around Denver by yourself this late at night?"

Trying to ignore the fact that her husband was naked beneath the sheet, Agnes said, "I needed to think. Alone."

"Are you finished thinking? Alone?"

It was several moments before she nodded. It was several more moments before she said, "I almost bought a train ticket to California. Two things stopped me. The first thing was the fact that I didn't have any money."

"And the second?"

Agnes did not miss the desire in his eyes. She swallowed. "I- I want to be your wife." When Nathaniel let the sheet fall to his lap, she quickly added, "In name only."

Nathaniel shook his head. "You will be my wife in every sense of the word."

That sounds rather medieval," she said, incredulously.

"I'm an old-fashioned man, Agnes."

"I know nothing about you."

"That makes two of us." He stared up at her for a moment before continuing, "We will talk later. Right now, I want to make love to you."

Agnes couldn't breathe. "You are definitely no man of God," she whispered.

"You have no idea."

When Agnes wrinkled her brow, Nathaniel continued, "I am a man, Agnes. Being a minister is just my occupation." He held out his hand. "Will you be my wife in every sense of the word?" Smiling a strained smile, he continued, "If you don't want to be my wife in every sense of the word, I will give you the money to buy a one-way ticket to California."

CHAPTER TWELVE

Who Am I To Judge?

Agnes slowly sat down on the edge of the bed.

With the backs of his fingers, Nathaniel gently caressed one round cheek.

Agnes closed her eyes, giving in to the sensation of his touch.

Although he was only caressing her cheek, it felt as if her entire body was being caressed.

"Does this feel good?" Nathaniel softly asked her.

Agnes could only nod.

Nathaniel pulled his wife against his sheet-covered body, and kissed her.

At first, Agnes tried to fight against his passionate assault. But when she realized Nathaniel would never hurt her, and how much she wanted him, she let his passion take her.

Although inexperienced, Agnes' kiss moved him like no other ever had. Cradling her face in his hands, he deepened the kiss.

When Nathaniel's tongue gently touched hers, Agnes quickly pulled away.

"I didn't mean to frighten you," he gently said.

"You- You didn't frighten me," Agnes lied. "You just took me by surprise."

Nathaniel smiled at what he knew was a white lie. "May I kiss you again?"

Agnes stared at him for a moment before nodding.

This time, when Nathaniel's tongue touched hers, she relished the taste of him. How could a man of God kiss like this? How could a man of God taste so delicious?

So sinfully delicious.

When Nathaniel lowered her to the bed, he gently brushed her dark hair back from her face, and softly asked, "Do you know what I'm going to do? What we're going to do?"

"I'm not as innocent as you think, Nathaniel."

When he wrinkled his dark brow, she blushed, and quickly assured him that she was a virgin.

"My friends told me what happens between a man and a woman. While I don't know everything, I know enough." She stared at him for a moment before asking, "Would it have mattered?"

"While a minister prefers his wife to be virginal, no, it wouldn't have mattered. Who am I to judge?"

"What does that mean?"

"Nothing," Nathaniel quickly said. He lowered his head, and kissed her chin, and then moved to her neck.

Agnes stared up at the dark ceiling, wondering what he had meant. But when he began to undress her, she lost all train of thought, and surrendered wholeheartedly to him.

YOU MURDERED ME, NICK!

Just before dawn

Nathaniel's body glistened with sweat as he was pulled deeper into his all-to-real nightmare.

He suddenly found himself in a sepia replica of the woods that surrounded his past home outside St. Louis, Missouri. Despite the coloring of his dream, he vividly remembered the true colors of this specific memory.

It was a perfect spring day. Nary a cloud marred the clear, blue sky. The sun was warm, and the birds were singing.

Despite such perfection, Nathaniel knew there was something terribly wrong. He knew what would await him inside the large farmhouse.

Nathaniel found himself entering the house, and walking toward the kitchen in slow motion.

He then found himself standing in the doorway, staring down at the dead body of his wife.

Suddenly, the corpse lifted her head from the pool of blood on the kitchen table, glared at him with accusing eyes, and exclaimed, "You murdered me, Nick! You will pay for what you have done!"

REVEALING THEIR PASTS IN THEIR OWN TIME

Nathaniel quickly sat up, feeling as if his heart would explode in his chest.

Agnes slowly sat up beside him, and put her arms around his sweaty body.

It took him several long moments before he calmed down.

Gently stroking her husband's slick back, Agnes softly said, "You had a nightmare, Nathaniel. Do you want to tell me about it?"

He shook his head.

Although Agnes felt hurt, she understood and hoped he would

tell her about his past in his own good time.

Of course, in order for him to do that, she would have to reveal her own past.

She laid her head on his shoulder, and closed her eyes.

Being Watched

Eleven of the clock that morning

Walking toward the train, Agnes glanced back, and frowned.

Glancing at her, Nathaniel asked, "What's wrong?"

Agnes looked at him. "I have the strangest feeling I'm being watched. I had that same feeling the day I defended Mr. and Mrs. Jebejian." She frowned again. Had Rabbi Kuhn found her?

After helping Agnes onto the train, Nathaniel took a quick glance around the Denver station. Although he did not see anyone suspicious, he, too, had the feeling of being watched.

Ralph Cutter had come for him.

When would the bastard finally make his move?

The New Mrs. West

Ralph Cutter watched as the newlyweds boarded the train to Thunder Mountain.

Nick West's new wife sure was a beauty.

Not to mention voluptuous.

And fiery.

Tallulah West had been a skinny milquetoast. He had gotten more pleasure out of putting a bullet in her head than he had out of fucking her.

Although he wondered what the new Mrs. West would be like in bed, killing Nick was the only thing that truly mattered to him.

No.

There was one other person he would enjoy getting revenge on.

Maggie.

CHAPTER THIRTEEN

WHY IS IT...?

Thunder Mountain, Colorado
January 7, 1881

Entering the house, Edith and Callie hugged Agnes.

"Congratulations!" Callie warmly exclaimed.

Smiling, Agnes said, "Thank you, Callie."

Standing behind them, Edith noticed that Agnes' smile did not extend to her eyes. Something was wrong.

The three women made their way into the kitchen. The warm scents of food being prepared enticed them.

"You are going to make Reverend Weston one happy husband," Callie said.

Agnes blushed.

Edith and Callie hid their smiles behind their hands. By the way Agnes' cheeks flamed, they guessed she wasn't thinking about food.

While Agnes prepared cups of coffee for them, Callie watched her for a moment before saying, "I'm sorry, Agnes."

Agnes looked at her, and smiled. "I should be the one apologizing, Callie."

Callie smiled, and placed her hand over Agnes'. "You are a true heroine, doing what you did."

"I don't feel like a heroine. If I could turn back the clock, I would still defend Mr. and Mrs. Jebejian. But I paid a heavy price."

"What heavy price did you pay?" Edith asked. "You married a wonderful man."

"At the time, I didn't know I would be marrying a wonderful man. I thought I would have to leave town."

Callie was quiet for a moment before asking, "Why did you run away, Agnes?"

When Agnes and Edith looked at her, Callie quickly added, "What you tell us will not go beyond this room." Smiling, she continued, "I'm just beginning to understand that friends are more important to me than making a profit from someone's secrets."

Agnes took a sip of hot coffee, and then said, "I ran away from an arranged marriage to an abusive killer. What made it all the more terrible was the fact that he was a Rabbi. A Jewish man of God."

"Why is it that you can tell your friends about your past, but you cannot tell your own husband?"

Agnes quickly turned around to find Nathaniel standing in the doorway to the kitchen. Her heart sank at the look on his face, and at the knowledge that she hadn't been able to tell him her secret.

She quickly hurried past him, and ran upstairs to their bedroom.

GIVING HER THE TRUTH

An hour later

Nathaniel entered the bedchamber to find his wife staring out the window at the late snowy afternoon.

"You are my husband in name only."

"We consummated our marriage, Agnes. We are man and wife in every sense of the word."

"Except love."

"Is love important to you, Agnes?"

Agnes turned to face him. "Isn't love important to everyone?"

"You don't love me."

"Why won't you tell me about your past? What was your nightmare about the other night?"

"If you don't love me, then why does it matter?"

Agnes stared at him for a moment. "You are not a cold-hearted man, Nathaniel. Why are you pretending to be one?"

"You don't know anything about me, Agnes."

"I'm trying to learn! Why won't you let me?"

"You'll hate me when you learn the truth about me."

"The other night, you said, 'Who am I to judge?' It is my turn to ask that question."

Nathaniel looked at her, took a deep breath, and then blew it out. If she wanted the truth, he would give it to her.

CHAPTER FOURTEEN

THERE'S SOMETHING ROTTEN IN THE STATE OF DENMARK

January 9, 1881

That Sunday, the parishioners gathered outside the locked church.

Callie had been assigned the task of letting everyone know that Reverend and Mrs. Weston were "bedridden with colds".

No one could know that Agnes had left her husband, and was staying with Zachary and Edith.

"I will take them some hot chicken noodle soup," Hannah said.

"No!" Callie quickly said. When everyone looked at her, she quickly added, "I've been taking care of their meals. Hannah, you're expecting. You don't want to risk your health."

Viola Main stepped forward, and said, "There's something rotten in the State of Denmark."

Forcing herself to keep her cool, Callie said, "There's nothing rotten anywhere, Mrs. Main."

When Viola Main opened her mouth once again to contradict her, Josiah Porter announced, "Folks, Miss Cooper has not told you the truth!"

While Callie stared incredulously at him, everyone else stared at her.

"Miss Cooper did not know how else to tell you that Reverend and Mrs. Weston want to be left alone," Josiah continued. Smiling a wicked smile, he asked, "Do you understand my meaning?"

While polite chuckles rippled through the crowd, Callie mouthed, "Thank you."

Josiah Porter nodded, and placed his arm around his wife.

Viola Main did not miss this brief interaction. There was, indeed, something very rotten in the State of Denmark.

Why Did It Hurt So Much?

That evening

"Who am I to judge?"
 "I used to be an outlaw."
 "I refuse to be married to a violent killer!"

No matter how hard he tried, Nathaniel could not eat his supper. Pushing his plate away, he stood, opened the back door, and walked outside. He looked up at the starry sky.

The two most important women in his life had left him.

Although Tallulah's leaving had not been by choice, she had tired of their outlaw lifestyle.

And of him.

Although Tallulah had been murdered, Agnes walking out on him had been more painful. He had told her his secret, and she had treated him with contempt.

Love had never played a part in his relationship with Tallulah. Although she had been his wife, their marriage, as it was with Agnes, had been a marriage of convenience.

Nathaniel had never wished Tallulah dead. He had truly mourned her loss, and her companionship, despite the fact that she had betrayed him.

With Agnes, Nathaniel did not know what he felt. He had wanted her from the moment he had met her. Did that constitute love?

Or was it just lust?

Whatever it was, he had never felt that way with Tallulah. While Tallulah had been a pleasure in bed, she had been nothing like Agnes.

Although love might not play a factor in their relationship, Agnes made him feel things he had never felt before.

Good.

Happy.

Whole.

Nathaniel looked down at the dark ground. He had trusted Agnes with his secret, and she had treated him like the dirt beneath her feet.

Why did it hurt so much?

Maybe because he truly loved her?

Support

Later that evening

"Who am I to judge?"

"I used to be an outlaw."

"I refuse to be married to a violent killer!"

Zachary stepped out onto the porch, and sat down beside Agnes on the porch swing.

"Are you cold?"

Agnes shook her head. She felt nothing.

"You didn't touch your supper."

"I wasn't hungry."

Zachary placed his hand on her arm, and said, "Agnes, you need to support your husband."

Agnes turned to stare incredulously at him for a moment before asking, "Do you support your wife, Zachary?"

"This is not about Edith and me."

Ignoring him, she said, "We both married outlaws. We both hate the fact that we married outlaws."

Zachary frowned. "I love my wife very much, Agnes."

"You can love someone, and still despise who they are."

"Do you love Nathaniel?"

"That's not important!" Agnes snapped.

"Do you love Nathaniel?" Zachary repeated.

Agnes was silent for several long moments before whispering, "Yes."

A single tear slid down her cheek.

"Then you need to support your husband."

Agnes stared at him for a long moment before finally saying, "And you need to support your wife, Zachary."

I Heed Your Warning, My Lovely Little Outlaw.

Later that night

Edith looked up from her book when her husband entered their bedchamber.

"What book are you reading now?" Zachary asked her.

"*A Tale of Two Cities.*"

"Isn't Jenny a little too young for that?"

"It's for my own reading enjoyment. Next up is *The Scarlet Letter.*"

"*The Scarlet Letter* doesn't sound like the type of book Marjorie Main would allow in her library."

"I was quite surprised when I saw it. And yet, she still frowned upon my choice of reading material." She stared down at the book, and softly continued, "After all, I am a scarlet woman."

Angry that Edith would dare to call herself a scarlet woman,

Zachary sat down on the edge of the bed, and took the book from her.

It was several long seconds before Edith finally looked up at him. He could see that she was forcing herself not to cry. Gently caressing her cheek, he softly said, "I'm sorry."

"For what?" Edith whispered.

"For making you believe that I'm ashamed of being married to you because of your past."

Edith frowned. "Aren't you?"

Zachary shook his head. "I could never be ashamed of you, Sweetheart. I just hate that your past, in the form of Ralph Cutter, is coming back to haunt you. That's why I will be taking you, Jenny, and our unborn child up to the cabin." Taking her face in his hands, he said, "Do not argue with me, Edith."

Edith smiled. Saucily, she said, "I like it when you're bossy."

Zachary laughed, and kissed her.

Smiling, Edith said, "I love you, Zachary. But if you ever keep your true feelings from me again, I will shoot you where the sun don't shine!"

With lust, and love, in his black eyes, Zachary said, "I heed your warning, my lovely little outlaw."

She laughed.

Kissing her, he lowered her into the bedding.

Violence, Religion, And Love

Late that night

Agnes opened the bedroom door to find herself face-to-face with a pistol. "Since when do ministers carry guns?"

"Since they are ex-outlaws, and have to be prepared for unexpected visitors." Nathaniel carefully placed the pistol in the drawer of the bedside table, and pushed it shut.

"I despise guns."

"Did you come here to continue your fight, Agnes?"

"My fight?"

"Since you're unwilling to accept my past, it's your fight."

"Your past is going to get you killed, Nathaniel."

"Do you have more faith in Ralph Cutter than you do in your own husband?"

"I don't have any faith."

Nathaniel frowned. "You don't believe in God?"

"Religion is a curse."

"I once felt the same exact way. And then I found God." He

looked at her for a moment. "Why did you marry me, Agnes?"

"I had no choice."

"You had many choices, Agnes. Why did you marry me?"

The silence was deafening. After several long moments, she finally whispered, "Because I love you."

Nathaniel tossed back the covers, and got out of bed.

Agnes could not tear her gaze from his naked body.

His magnificent, naked body.

How could a minister be so damned attractive?

Because he was no man of God.

He was an ex-outlaw.

And at this very moment, she didn't give a damn.

Nathaniel looked at his beautiful wife for a moment before taking her in his arms, and kissing her. He then stared into her dark eyes, and seductively asked, "Will you let me make love to you?"

Agnes could only nod. But when he picked her up in his strong arms, she softly asked, "Making love is about love, isn't it?"

Nathaniel could only nod. Kissing her, he carried her to the bed, and lowered her into the bedding. Continuing to kiss her, he did not waste any time in taking off her clothes.

When his wife was completely naked, the look on his face showed his feelings.

Not to mention another part of his body.

Although tall, she was voluptuous, with large, full breasts. He had a sudden image of those breasts nourishing the babies they would have together.

Would he live long enough to have babies with her?

Gently caressing one breast, Nathaniel lowered his mouth, and caressed the soft flesh with his lips.

Agnes' dark eyes fluttered closed, and her breath came in short pants as she gave in to the sensations coursing through her. She finally knew, without a doubt, she had found love. Nathaniel might be an ex-outlaw, but at this very moment, that didn't matter.

All that mattered was love.

Agnes slowly opened her eyes when Nathaniel entered her body. She gazed into his eyes for a long moment before putting her arms around him, and gently caressed his back and buttocks.

Although his wife's caresses were innocent, Nathaniel felt as if his entire body was being caressed by hot flames. If Ralph Cutter's pistol didn't kill him, Agnes' touch surely would.

Nathaniel cupped Agnes' face in his hands, forcing her to look at him. "Do you truly love me, Agnes?"

Tears streamed down her face. "Yes," she whispered.

Nathaniel smiled. Kissing her, he whispered, "You are not alone, Sweetheart." He stared at her for a long moment before finally saying, "I love you, Agnes."

Alone

Morning

The morning sunlight flooded the room, waking Nathaniel from a deep sleep.

He reached for Agnes, only to find he was alone.

She had left him.

Although she loved him, she did not want to be married to him.

An ex-outlaw.

Unmoving, he simply stared at the sunlit shadows dancing on the wall.

CHAPTER FIFTEEN

Why Can't You Be Nathaniel's Wife?

Up on Thunder Mountain
January 14, 1881

Sitting on a tree trunk, Agnes stared out at the breathtaking view of Thunder Mountain.

Having returned to the Scalen household from her passionate, loving night with her husband, Agnes had asked if she could go up to the cabin with them. Although Zachary and Edith had warmly welcomed her company, she knew they were not happy that she was leaving her husband.

Despite the chill of the early morning air, Agnes did not feel cold. She felt nothing but the terrible ache in her heart.

The sound of a twig snapping in the deafening silence caused Agnes to startle, and quickly stand.

At the sight of Nathaniel's friend, Damien, she breathed a sigh of relief.

Damien smiled warmly, and said, "I didn't mean to frighten you, Mrs. Weston."

"Please, call me Agnes."

"Your nerves must be on edge, what with Ralph Cutter in town."

Agnes frowned. "Ralph Cutter's in town?"

"I thought you knew. Nathaniel told me you felt like you were being watched."

"By someone else. How do you know he's in town?"

Damien stared incredulously at her for a moment before saying, with a smile, "I'm an Indian."

Agnes blushed. "I'm sorry. I know that Indians have special skills. So, Ralph Cutter was, indeed, watching Nathaniel and me? Why didn't Nathaniel tell me?"

"Does it matter?"

Agnes just stared at him.

Damien did not miss the sadness in her dark eyes. After several long moments, he finally said, "I only just told him last night." Several more moments passed before he continued, "Agnes, Nathaniel needs you."

"Nathaniel can take care of himself."

"How can you be so cold?"

"Nathaniel is an ex-outlaw."

"So is Edith."

Agnes frowned. "We are not talking about Edith. We are talking about Nathaniel."

Ignoring her, Damien continued, "You are friends with Edith. Why can't you be Nathaniel's wife?"

Why was Damien doing this to her? Why was he making her see that what she was doing to Nathaniel, to herself, was wrong? Cold.

"A relationship between friends is different than a relationship between a man and his wife."

"Only when it comes to intimacy." He smiled when Agnes blushed again. Although he was angry with this woman for daring to hurt his friend, he liked her. "If Edith's past came back to haunt her, which it has, you are still her friend. Why can't you still be Nathaniel's friend? Why can't you still be his wife?"

Agnes turned, and started to walk away.

Taking a deep breath, Damien said, "When I found Nathaniel, I could have left him for dead. In fact, I wanted to leave him for dead. I even wanted to scalp him. But I didn't."

Agnes turned to face him. "What?"

"Nathaniel and I had been enemies. It was only a matter of time before he killed me. Before he killed my people. Before I killed him. When I found him, barely alive, I made the risky decision to nurse him back to health. We became friends. When he found God, he taught me about God. I didn't just risk my life to help him, I risked the lives of my people." Damien was silent for a moment before quietly saying, "He is a good man."

Agnes watched as he walked away.

CHAPTER SIXTEEN

Why Hadn't She Believed?

Brooklyn Heights, Brooklyn, New York
January 17, 1881

Deep in prayer, Rebecca's eyes flew open at the sound of Rabbi Kuhn's loud, argumentative voice. Thank goodness she was seated behind a curtain. She did not want him to know she was there.

Although the temple's acoustics made it hard to understand what Rabbi Kuhn and the head rabbi were arguing about, what she did hear made her dark brown eyes widen in shock.

Pressing her hand to her mouth, Rebecca closed her eyes. Dear God, why hadn't she believed in her own sister?

Tears slid down her face.

We Must Find Rachel Before He Does!

In shock, Rabbi Berezovsky asked, "How could we have been so blind?"

Cradling her infant son in her arms, Rebecca softly said, "I did not believe in my own sister." Whispering, she continued, "Only God knows where she is."

Angry, and scared, Rivkah Berezovsky exclaimed, "We must find Rachel before he does!"

Rabbi Berezovsky took his wife in his arms, and gently stroked her red hair. Her back.

Suddenly, his hand froze. His wife lifted her head, and stared into his eyes. He stared into hers.

Rebecca did not miss this interaction between her parents.

Staring down at her beautiful son, she smiled.

Her parents had just fallen in love.

MARRIAGE ANNOUNCEMENT

January 19, 1881

Agnes was in Thunder Mountain, Colorado. And she was married to a minister.

Sharon Berezovsky's heart skipped a million beats as she reread the newspaper article, and stared at the photo of her sister and her husband. Agnes was alive and well. And married to a minister.

Grabbing the newspaper, she quickly hurried to her father's study.

TONIGHT!

Thunder Mountain, Colorado
January 23, 1881-Seven of the clock in the morning

Nathaniel entered the kitchen, and stopped dead in his tracks.
Ralph Cutter had been here.
Knifed to his kitchen door was a single sheet of white paper.
A single word had been written in blood.
Ralph Cutter's blood.
TONIGHT!

CHAPTER SEVENTEEN

ORDER

Eleven of the clock that morning

Once again, the residents of Thunder Mountain, Colorado found the church doors locked. This time, there was no one to explain why Reverend Weston was not preaching this morning.

There was a piece of white paper taped in the center of the two double doors. Written in Reverend Weston's meticulous printing was the order, "Do not come into town until further notice. Stay inside, and keep your doors and windows locked. Stay away from the windows. May God be with you. I'm sorry I deceived you. Reverend Weston."

Most of the residents fled. Only a select few, like Mayor and Mrs. Main, stayed, and tried to answer questions.

Callie made her way to her office, and sat down at her desk. She positioned her fingers above the keys of her typewriter.

But she couldn't type.

Not because she didn't have enough information, but because she simply didn't want to.

No matter what he had done, Reverend Weston was still her friend.

She could not, would not, hurt her friend with gossip.

Even if it was the truth.

TOWN 9 PREPARE TO DIE!!!

Three of the clock that afternoon

Someone pounded on the front door, waking Nathaniel from a sound sleep.

Slowly making his way downstairs, he unlocked the front door, and opened it.

No one was there.

Glancing down, Nathaniel noticed a note knifed to the welcome mat.

Written, once again, in Ralph Cutter's blood, were the words TOWN 9 PREPARE TO DIE!!!

Nathaniel closed his eyes.

And prayed.

CHAPTER EIGHTEEN

Thou Shalt Not Kill

Nine of the clock that night

All was silent.

And, except for the street lamps, all was dark.

Nathaniel stood in the middle of the street, peering into the darkness.

When would Ralph Cutter show himself?

Why didn't the bastard just kill him, and get it over with?

It was as if the bastard had read his thoughts.

Suddenly appearing out of nowhere, Ralph Cutter said, "I like to make my victims suffer."

"I have been suffering for a long time, Cutter. Kill me now!"

"You haven't suffered long enough, West."

"It's *Weston!*"

Smiling evilly, Ralph Cutter said, "You can pretend all you want, West. A leopard never changes its spots."

Nathaniel softly said, "God is on my side."

Ignoring him, Ralph Cutter asked, "Why haven't you made the first move, West? What are you waiting for?"

"Thou shalt not kill."

Ralph Cutter rolled his eyes. "You want to kill me, West. You want to put a bullet in me for daring to betray you. For daring to fuck and murder your wife."

Nathaniel's shaking hand touched his gun.

The gun he hadn't touched since finding God.

Ralph Cutter's hand moved to his gun. "Shoot me, Nick." Suddenly furious, he roared, "Shoot me for daring to fuck and murder that scrawny, little bitch! Shoot me, you goddamned sonofabitch!"

Before Cutter could blink, or take another breath, a single bullet hit him right between the eyes. He only had a split second to realize he was dead before he hit the ground.

Nathaniel stood there for several long moments.
And then, he fell to his knees.
And sobbed.

CHAPTER NINETEEN

WHAT ABOUT LOVE?

Hunter Lord's saloon was filled beyond capacity.

While Mayor and Mrs. Main, and others, were demanding answers, Callie sat down beside Nathaniel, and handed him a glass of water. "I thought water would be better, under the circumstances," she said.

His hand shaking, Nathaniel lifted the glass to his lips, and gulped the cold water down. He then stared at the empty glass for a moment before whispering, "Thank you." Several long moments passed before he was able to look at her. "Aren't you going to ask me questions for your article?"

Callie shook her head. "No."

Nathaniel knew what that simple word meant. And yet, he had to ask, "Why not?"

Callie smiled. "You're my friend."

Nathaniel swallowed, and quickly looked away. Tears formed in his eyes, and he fought hard to keep them from falling.

Mayor and Viola Main made their way to his table. "You owe everyone an explanation!" Mayor Main demanded.

"Now is not the time to question Reverend Weston," Callie told them.

Glaring down at the nosy reporter, Viola Main snapped, "Stay out of this, Miss Cooper!" Shifting her gaze to the minister, she demanded, "Answer our questions, Reverend Weston!"

Nathaniel continued to stare at his empty glass for a moment before handing it to Callie, and standing. He glanced around the saloon. Swallowing, he said, "I have deceived all of you. Before I became your minister, I was a mean outlaw. I was right up there with Jesse James. I robbed banks, and I killed people. I knew no other way of life. I know there is no excuse for what I did, but I was born into a life of crime. My father was an outlaw, and my mother was a prostitute. I married a woman who ended up betraying me with an ex-partner of mine. But no matter what she did, she did not deserve what Ralph Cutter did to her. She paid the ultimate price for a life of crime. I paid the price by

-64-

going to prison. I thought I was going to hang for my crimes. Instead, I was released. Ralph Cutter was furious. He vowed revenge. I ran. I became ill, and almost died. And then, I found God." Long moments passed before he continued. "I'm not asking for understanding or forgiveness. I'm asking for the chance to live the rest of my life in peace and goodness. Maybe even a little happiness."

"What about love?"

Nathaniel turned to stare at the woman in front of the swinging doors.

Agnes.

His wife.

He wanted to go to her. He wanted to take her in his arms. He wanted to hold her. He wanted to kiss her.

He wanted to love her.

But she had deeply hurt him by leaving him.

Without a by-your-leave, Nathaniel quickly pushed through the crowd, hurried up the stairs, and exited the saloon through the back entrance.

Make Me!

Agnes entered Nathaniel's bedroom.

No.

Not Nathaniel's bedroom.

Their bedroom.

Not turning away from the window, Nathaniel exclaimed, "Get the hell out of here, Agnes!"

Although hurt, she jokingly said, "For a man of God, you have a foul mouth."

Nathaniel turned to face her. Agnes' heart went out to him when she saw that he was crying.

Walking toward him, Agnes said, "I will not get the hell out of here, Nathaniel."

Glaring at her, he demanded, "Where were you when I needed you?"

"If you had told me the truth, I would have been right by your side."

"I told you the truth, and you ran."

"I ran because you told me you were an ex-outlaw. You didn't tell me what you told everyone else."

"Would it have made a difference, Agnes? You obviously have an affliction for men of violence."

"My parents were going to force marriage to a man I didn't love. Although he was a rabbi, he was no man of God. I believed there was something twisted about him, but my own family did not believe me. When this man of God murdered an innocent beggar, he showed no remorse. I came to Thunder Mountain so I would be safe. I know it's only a matter of time before he finds me. Only, his finding me won't be as deadly as it was when Ralph Cutter found you. I can handle Rabbi Jacob Kuhn. I cannot handle your past."

"My past died with Ralph Cutter."

"God only knows how many enemies you have, Nathaniel. There's no doubt they'll come riding into town, seeking revenge."

"That's a chance I'll have to take."

"Is that a chance you want me to take? What if one of them decides to murder me? I refuse to end up like your first wife."

Nathaniel just stared at her for a moment before saying, "You should have been an actress, Agnes. You have quite a fondness for being dramatic."

Agnes slapped him hard across the face.

Nathaniel glared at her for several long moments before exclaiming, once again, "Get the hell out of here, Agnes!"

"Make me!"

Before Nathaniel could blink, before he could take another breath, Agnes threw herself against him, and passionately kissed him.

CHAPTER TWENTY

Of Love.

Just before dawn

After making love all night, they lay naked in each other's arms, and talked about their pasts.

Gently stroking his wife's dark hair back from her damp face, he asked, "Why are you staying?"

"Because I love you," she softly said.

"Why did you leave me? Was it truly because of my past?"

Agnes started to turn away from him, but Nathaniel wouldn't let her. Pulling her against his hard, naked body, he asked again, "Was it truly because of my past?"

Agnes whispered, "I was afraid."

"Of me?"

Agnes was silent for a moment before saying, "Of love." She closed her eyes.

"Of love?"

When Agnes slowly opened her eyes, she saw he was watching her.

Smiling sheepishly, she said, "All my life, I prayed for love. I prayed someone would fall in love with me. When my prayers came true, I became frightened. It had nothing to do with you, and everything to do with me, Nathaniel. While it's true that a life of violence scares me, I cannot imagine my life without you. I cannot imagine my life without your love." Tears streamed down her face, and her voice broke when she whispered, "I love you."

Nathaniel gently kissed her. Rolling over so she was on top of him, his kiss became passionate.

Although terrified, she was bold. Sitting up, she straddled her husband, and looked down at him. Her fingers began to innocently caress his magnificent, bare chest.

Grinning from ear to ear, Nathaniel said, "In this position, I am definitely no man of God."

"This is one time I wouldn't mind playing outlaw and captor,"

Agnes said coyly.

Nathaniel laughed. "Do you want to be the outlaw?"

Agnes' dark eyes turned as black as sin. The innocent suddenly became the seductress.

Nathaniel's manhood grew harder. And larger.

Agnes swallowed.

Gently, and boldly, caressing the powerful instrument, she said, in a low, seductive voice, "I want to be the captor."

Nathaniel was a goner.

BOOT HILL

January 25, 1881-Seven of the clock in the morning

Nathaniel, Agnes, Zachary, Edith, and Damien attended Ralph Cutter's burial on Boot Hill.

During the service, Agnes put her hand on her husband's arm, and quietly asked, "Are you all right?"

Nathaniel could only nod as he watched the undertaker's assistants lower Ralph Cutter's coffin into the hole.

When the quick funeral was over, Nathaniel said, "I need to go to the church to prepare for tomorrow's meeting."

"You need to get some rest, Nathaniel," Agnes gently said.

"I can rest once my past is finally laid to rest," Nathaniel said. Without a by-your-leave, he left the degenerate cemetery.

Edith took Agnes' gloved hand in hers.

Agnes just stared down at the icy ground.

FUCK!

Calico, Kansas
January 25, 1881

"Fuck!" Sheriff Bill Anderson roared.

Ignoring the curious stares from passersby, he stared down at the telegram in his hand. Ralph Cutter was dead.

Stomping the icy ground with his boot, he roared, once again, "Fuck!" The stupid fuck had never been able to do anything right!

Sheriff Anderson hurried down the street toward his office. He had to come up with a new plan. He had to find the one person who knew how to do his job.

He would not rest until he made sure Caroline and Maggie paid for what they'd done to him.

CHAPTER TWENTY-ONE

Resign

Thunder Mountain, Colorado
January 26, 1881

The meeting on whether or not to dismiss Reverend Weston from his ministerial duties had started out pleasant enough, but ended up turning into a full-fledged war.

Sitting in the back of the church, so as not to distract her husband, Agnes wondered why Nathaniel was not defending himself. Why was he allowing people like Mayor and Viola Main to get the best of him?

Slapping a blank sheet of white paper in front of Nathaniel, Viola Main ordered, "Give us your resignation!"

Nathaniel stared down at the blank sheet for several long moments. Picking up an ink-filled quill, he began to write.

Quickly standing, Agnes shouted, "Don't give them your resignation, Nathaniel!"

Everyone turned in their seats. Nathaniel put down the quill, and focused his attention on his wife.

Swallowing, Agnes continued, "Don't give these people what they want, Nathaniel. You are a good man. Even when you were bad, you were good. How can a bad man become friends with an enemy and his people? How can a bad man find God? How can a bad man protect the people in this town? How can a bad man love a Jewish woman? You never once condemned me for being a Jew. For not believing in Jesus. You love God. You love being a minister. Why must you give up being what you love because Mayor and Viola Main tell you to?" Glaring at the older woman, she exclaimed, "Mrs. Main, you can kiss my Jewish ass!"

For several long moments, there was complete silence.

And then, Nathaniel burst into laughter.

Seconds later, almost everyone else laughed with him.

When Nathaniel held out his hand to her, Agnes quickly hurried down the aisle, and threw herself into his arms. Almost everyone clapped and cheered, especially when they kissed.

Reluctantly breaking the kiss, Nathaniel looked down at her. Grinning, he said, "Thank you for your unconventional support, Wife. Never, in a million years, will I forget it. But, I must resign."

Before Agnes could say another word, Nathaniel put one finger to her lips, and said, "Damien has offered me a position. I will be preaching to his people."

Agnes smiled.

"We want you to teach the children about God," Nathaniel told her.

Frowning, Agnes said, "Nathaniel, I don't believe in Jesus. How can I teach something I don't believe in?"

"We want you to teach the children what you do believe in. Will you accept the position?"

Tears formed in Agnes' eyes. "Yes," she whispered.

Nathaniel lowered his head, and kissed her again.

"I hate to interrupt such a touching scene, but we need your resignation, Mr. Weston," Viola Main said.

Reluctantly breaking the kiss, Nathaniel grabbed the quill, and quickly signed his name. Picking up the paper, he threw it at the older woman. "It's Reverend Weston, Mrs. Main! Now, if you'll excuse me, I'm going to celebrate with my wife."

Taking Agnes' hand in his, they walked up the aisle. When they got to the double doors, Nathaniel turned back, and said, "By the way, Mrs. Main, when you're done kissing my wife's Jewish ass, you can kiss my Christian one!"

Amidst the clapping and cheering, husband and wife hurried out of the building, and quickly made their way home to "celebrate".

CHAPTER TWENTY-TWO

MISS MABEL'S CONFESSION

January 29, 1881-Eleven of the clock in the morning

Agnes exited *Thunder Mountain General Store,* and came face-to-face with Miss Mabel.

When Agnes tried to walk around the bigoted woman, Miss Mabel stopped her with the touch of her hand, and said, "I'm sorry, Mrs. Weston."

Agnes stared at her for a moment before asking, "Why are you apologizing for being a bigot?"

"Mrs. Weston, I am not a bigot!"

"You could have fooled me."

"You're not making this easy!"

"Why should I make this easy for you?"

Miss Mabel stared at her for a moment before asking, "How can I be a bigot when I'm Jewish?"

Agnes stared incredulously at her for a long moment. "You're Jewish?"

"Unlike you, I was too scared, and still am, to admit to such a thing."

"I was very scared, Miss Mabel. I still am."

Smiling, Miss Mabel said, "Yes, but you have chutzpah."

Agnes laughed. "I do, don't I? Thank you for your apology, Miss Mabel. By the way, please call me Agnes."

"Only if you call me Mabel."

The two women smiled at each other.

"Agnes, I need to ask a favor of you."

A little hesitant, Agnes asked, "What?"

"Will you teach me how to make a pie for tonight's supper?"

Agnes smiled. "Give me two hours."

I Love You, Miss Mabel.

As Mabel made her way toward the boardinghouse, Cowboy Dave stepped into her path. Trying to walk around him, his words stopped her dead in her tracks.

"I love you, Miss Mabel. Marry me."

Mabel stared at him for several moments before asking, "Are you drunk? Insane?"

Cowboy Dave laughed. "I've been asking myself those questions ever since I decided that I love you, and want to marry you."

Mabel brushed past him. Suddenly, she stopped, turned back around, and said, "By the way, Cowboy Dave, I'm Jewish. Does that matter?"

Without waiting for his answer, she walked away.

Found

Eight-fifteen in the evening

Agnes stood on the footbridge, staring down at the ice-covered stream.

Shivering, she took a deep breath of the fresh mountain air. She looked up at the night sky with a full moon and twinkling stars.

At the sound of footsteps, Agnes turned. Her dark eyes widened in fear.

Rabbi Jacob Kuhn had found her.

CHAPTER TWENTY-THREE

No Escape

"I'm here to take you home, Rachel."

Despite her fear, she glared at him, and exclaimed, "My name is Agnes!"

Quickly closing the distance between them, Rabbi Kuhn grabbed her arms.

To no avail, Agnes struggled to break free.

"You cannot escape from me this time!" Rabbi Kuhn exclaimed.

"That's what you think!"

Slowly lifting her leg, she quickly kneed him in the groin.

Although Rabbi Kuhn was in pain, he did not let go of her arms when he lost his balance, and fell over the side, crashing into the icy stream below.

CHAPTER TWENTY-FOUR

Drowning

Agnes sank to the bottom of the stream.
    She had fought hard to break free of the heavy weight of her skirts.
    Looking up, she focused on the sight of Rabbi Kuhn's floating body.
    And then, darkness claimed her.

CHAPTER TWENTY-FIVE

Saving Agnes

Nathaniel jumped into the icy water, and quickly pulled Agnes out. Holding his wife's body in his arms, he slapped her back several times.

Coughing up water, Agnes opened her eyes to see her husband kneeling above her. Suddenly, she began to cry.

Quietly swearing under his breath, Nathaniel carefully pulled his wife into his arms, and held her tightly against him.

Cowboy Dave knelt down beside the pair, and draped warm blankets around them. Damien lowered himself into the icy stream to fetch Rabbi Kuhn's body.

Agnes tried to look, but Nathaniel wouldn't let her. "You don't need to look, Sweetheart."

Barely able to speak, she asked, "Wh- What happened?"

"When both of you fell into the stream," Damien said, "he broke his neck."

"I almost drowned," Agnes whispered.

"Shh," Nathaniel soothed, gently stroking her wet hair.

"If it hadn't been for Damien, you might have. He was watching over you," Cowboy Dave told her.

Through her tears, Agnes smiled at the Indian, and then closed her eyes.

Carrying several blankets, Mabel stepped onto the footbridge.

"Thank you," Damien said, taking the blankets from her.

Mabel focused on Cowboy Dave, who was staring at her. Several long moments passed before she finally said, "Yes."

Smiling, Cowboy Dave pulled her into his arms, and kissed her.

Damien and Nathaniel looked at each other, and then back at Cowboy Dave and Miss Mabel. "Are we missing something?" Damien asked.

Breaking the kiss for a moment, Cowboy Dave said, "Miss Mabel and I are getting married." He resumed the kiss.

Agnes slowly opened her eyes, and whispered, "Congratulations."

After several minutes of congratulating the happy couple, Damien said, "I'll take the body to the undertaker."

"Damien," Agnes whispered, "tell the undertaker to send Rabbi Kuhn's body back to New York. No matter what he was, no matter what he did, his family deserves to give their son a proper burial."

Nathaniel looked at his wife with so much love, and whispered, "I love you so damned much."

Agnes smiled. "For a man of God, you have a foul mouth."

Nathaniel laughed.

And then, he kissed her.

CHAPTER TWENTY-SIX

TALLULAH'S BLESSING

January 30, 1881

Kneeling in front of the fireplace inside Damien's hogan, Nathaniel prayed for God's guidance.

"Dear Lord," he whispered, "please don't let me fail Damien and his people. Please don't let me fail Agnes. And," he swallowed hard, "please don't let me fail you."

Nathaniel stared into the flames of the fire for a moment before thinking about the dream he had had early that morning. In the dream, the ghost of his dead wife had stood before him, and he'd been frightened.

Taking a step toward him, the ghost of Tallulah had said, *"Do not be afraid, Nathaniel. I came here to tell you I never once blamed you for my murder. It is I who ask for your forgiveness. You changed for the better, and have a great life ahead of you filled with happiness, love, and many children. I also came to tell you that God has forgiven you. You will not fail Damien and his people. You will not fail Agnes. And, you will not fail God. You are blessed, Nathaniel. And you are whole."*

Tears formed in his eyes. He did not move for several long moments.

Suddenly, he felt God's healing power. His heart was no longer hardened.

Smiling, Nathaniel stood, and exited the hogan.

BLESSED AND WHOLE

Nathaniel could not believe his eyes.

He had expected Agnes, Damien, and Damien's people to attend the chilly outdoor service.

He had not expected Zachary, Edith, Callie, Cowboy Dave, Miss Mabel, Hunter, Rose, their employees, the Porter Family, the Rogers Family, the Pringle Family, Sheriff Main, Luke, Luke's dog,

Tater Bob, and Luke and Tater Bob's moonshine to attend.

True to Tallulah's words, he felt truly blessed.

And whole.

Family Reunion

Nathaniel and Agnes were warmly greeting everyone when Agnes' eyes widened in surprise. Standing before her was her family.

"Father," she whispered. "Mother." Sudden tears caused her voice to break when she continued, "I- I am so sorry."

"We are the ones who are sorry, Rachel," her father said. He stared at her for a moment before saying, "No. Not Rachel. Agnes." Pausing for several long moments, he continued, "We are sorry we didn't believe you. Can you ever forgive us?"

Tears streaming down her cheeks, Agnes threw herself into her father's arms. Her mother, Sharon, Joanna, and Rebecca, holding her infant son, joined in the family hug.

After several long moments, Agnes told her family everything that had happened.

"He wanted to marry you because he needed to pay off his gambling debts," Rebecca said. "Although the Kuhn Family is rich, we are richer. I overheard the head Rabbi telling Rabbi Kuhn he was going to be relieved of his position. Rabbi Kuhn threatened to expose his secrets."

"I commend you for having his body sent back to New York, Agnes," Sharon said. "I would have told the undertaker to throw him in an unmarked grave on Boot Hill."

Agnes looked up at her husband, then back at her family. "Father, Mother, Sharon, Joanna, Rebecca, this is Reverend Nathaniel Weston." Swallowing, she continued, "My husband." Taking a deep breath, she continued, "And an ex-outlaw."

Surprised, Nathaniel looked at her, and then smiled.

"We know," her mother said. "We read the newspaper article."

Staring at the minister for a moment, Rabbi Berezovsky smiled a warm smile, and then said, "Welcome to the family. Son."

Agnes smiled through her tears as she watched her family warmly welcome her husband into their fold. Making her way over to Rebecca, she met her beautiful infant nephew, and then quietly asked, "Did you leave your husband, Rebecca?"

After a few moments, Rebecca nodded. "I couldn't spend another moment in a loveless marriage. I will have to live in New York because of our son, but we will get a divorce when I return."

For the first time in a very long time, the two sisters warmly hugged each other.

"Agnes and I were supposed to go to the mountains for our honeymoon, but we can postpone our trip," Nathaniel said.

"Do not postpone your honeymoon!" Rivkah Berezovsky exclaimed. Looking lovingly into her husband's eyes, she said, "Love is very important."

Agnes did not miss the loving interaction between her parents. They had apparently fallen in love. Smiling, she said, "Nathaniel and I will be back in time for Sabbath supper on Friday." With hope in her dark eyes, she asked, "Will you still be here?"

"We are planning on staying for a couple of weeks," her father said. "Is that all right with you?"

Smiling, Agnes could only nod.

"You will be staying with us," Nathaniel told them.

"We don't want to impose," Rebecca said.

"You won't be imposing," Nathaniel said, putting his arm around his wife. "We're family."

Moonshine Wedding

When Cowboy Dave and Miss Mabel asked Nathaniel to marry them right after the service, he felt honored.

They were married in a short, but beautiful, ceremony.

Despite the last minute ceremony, the fiddle and banjo players gladly agreed to play their instruments. Some of the guests danced, and some toasted the happy couple, not to mention themselves, with moonshine.

Name Your Fool.

Standing near the edge of the forest, Rose watched Sheriff Main. "What is he doing here?"

Beside her, Hunter said, "It's obvious that Sheriff Main does not agree with his parents' politics."

Changing the subject, Rose said, "I wonder which fool Cupid's arrow will strike next."

"People who fall in love and get married are not fools, Rose."

"How much do you want to bet?"

Sighing, Hunter named his price.

"Name your fool," Rose said.

"Damien. Name your fool."

"You."

Hunter looked surprised. "Me? You'll surely lose this bet, Rose."

"This bet is my way of proving to you that love and marriage is a foolish thing. I know I'll lose. After all, people like us never fall in love and get married."

Not understanding why Rose's remark hurt, Hunter stared down at the icy ground.

Sunset Kiss

Up on Thunder Mountain
Sunset

Because of the surprise family reunion and wedding, Nathaniel and Agnes arrived at the mountain cabin in time to watch the sun go down behind the quaint town.

With tears in her dark eyes, Agnes said, "My parents fell in love."

"Just like you fell in love with someone like me," Nathaniel said.

Looking at her husband, she said, "I'm so sorry for hurting you, Nathaniel. For not standing beside you."

Nathaniel smiled. "You're standing beside me at this very moment. That's all that matters."

Agnes was silent for a moment before saying, "Nathaniel, I want to make a baby with you."

Nathaniel did not move or speak. Thinking he didn't want to do the same with her, she frowned.

Suddenly, Nathaniel took her in his arms, and spun her around.

Moments later, he realized what he was doing, and quickly put her down. "I'm sorry."

Agnes laughed. "You can spin me around all you want. But I'd prefer a kiss."

Smiling seductively, Nathaniel said, "It would be my pleasure to give you what you want. It would also be my pleasure to give you a baby."

As the sun set on such a beautiful, perfect day, the happy, loving couple kissed.

And kissed.

And kissed.

God had truly blessed them.

TO BE CONTINUED-

Coming Next

Book 3

THE DEVIL AND THE LORD

Danny's and Hunter's story

Amanda A. Brooks has been writing romance novels since the age of fourteen. In 2009, she decided to self-publish. Never without a book in her hand or bag, Amanda is an avid reader of romance and true crime (especially of stories from the 1960's.) She is always thinking of unique ideas for her stories. Amanda resides in Southern California.

This is the second book of a western romance series that Amanda has created. The first book, The Outlaw Schoolteacher - Edith, was released in December 2010, and she is working on her third book, The Devil and The Lord - Danny.

Made in the USA
Charleston, SC
28 June 2011